The
Black Stallion's
Ghost

The Black Stallion's Ghost

BY **WALTER FARLEY**

Illustrated by Angie Draper

B96510

RANDOM HOUSE   NEW YORK

For our Pam,
who brought Joy and Love to all those she touched
and who truly lived every day of her life

Contents

1 · The Ghost

The man was almost invisible against the backdrop of the dark velvet curtain. His tall figure was clothed completely in black and his hair and skin were black as well. He raised a large and corded hand, one capable of great strength, to touch the silver-gray body of the mare beside him. His hand was so light upon her that he might have been touching a ghost.

She responded to his touch by a slight fluttering of her ears. It was enough for him to know that she was expectant and ready to enter the ring. He parted the stage curtain a bit in order to see the spacious hall and audience on the other side.

It was his first visit to Stockholm, Sweden, and he was impressed. The hall was more like a theater than quarters for a circus. Festively illuminated, it was a pleasing sight on that bitter cold winter night. Red plush seats in ringside boxes and rear and side balconies rose to what seemed an incredible height. Every place was taken and all eyes were on the single ring where Davisio Castini and his bareback riding troupe were bringing their act to its finale.

The orchestra played a stirring march while the heavy horses thumped about the ring. The type did not appeal to him but he knew they had a place in the circus. He cared less for the feathered head plumes and jewel-studded breast collars they wore.

He touched his mare again and her ears pricked forward, awaiting his spoken command. There never would be any glittering ornaments on her, he promised himself. No plumes. No jewel-studded bridles. No colorful ribbons woven into her mane or tail. Nothing, not even a halter. By her movements alone she would overwhelm the audience.

He pressed closer against the curtain to avoid being seen. No emotion showed on his face; never had he allowed it to betray his feelings, in or out of the ring. Cold and masklike, and with deep-set unblinking black eyes, it resembled a piece of classic sculpture. Always he had sensed people's fear of him and, while he found it amusing, never attempted to change it.

The bareback act came to an end and there was a fanfare of drums from the orchestra, followed by a polite wave of applause from the large crowd. He listened and decided that, despite the air of festivity, the audience was as cold as the night outside.

Nervously, now that it was almost time for his mare to enter the ring, he removed a small gold figurine from his pocket and rubbed it gently. The growing warmth of the statuette in his large black hands gave him courage and confidence. He believed strongly in the powers of the small figurine, for his Haitian blood and heritage had made him more superstitious than most men.

The ringmaster, wearing frock coat and top hat, signaled him to be ready. *"Bientôt, ma cherie,"* he said quietly to his mare.

The fanfare of the trumpets cut the air once more. Then the shrill notes ended and the voice of the ringmaster rang through the spacious hall, as clear and commanding as the silver trumpets had been.

"Ladies and Gentlemen and Children," the ringmaster announced in Swedish, *"The Circus Heyer takes great pleasure in presenting The Ghost . . ."*

As the horseman listened to the introduction, he thought of the great number of languages in which he had heard it given. For more than ten years he had traveled with different circuses throughout Europe, as far east as Siberia as well as to all the British Isles.

He knew little Swedish but it made no difference since the introduction was always the same. Like the music which would follow, he had composed it himself, so he and his mare always felt at home in whatever country they played.

There was a long pause as the lights in the great hall dimmed until the audience sat in almost complete dark-

ness. This, too, he insisted upon wherever he played—
ten seconds, at the very minimum, to silence the spec-
tators and prepare them for the ethereal beauty of what
was to come.

He slipped the thin leather halter off the mare's head,
acutely aware of her readiness to obey every cue. He had
no doubt that she looked forward to the gala stage on
the other side of the curtain and the elegant audience
that would be watching her.

The ringmaster had moved to the orchestra pit, leaving the ring in total darkness. *"The Ghost,"* his introduction continued, *"a god-horse, one no longer earth-
bound but of dancing fire, a winged Pegasus . . ."*

The man holding the mare would have preferred it if
the introduction had ended there. He wanted nothing
more except complete silence and the darkness, followed
by the first haunting notes of the music. However, the
owner of the Circus Heyer, like most of the others he
had worked for, insisted that his name be mentioned
since it was familiar to circus audiences throughout the
world. He had given up arguing that it was only the
mare's performance that mattered.

*". . . A supreme exhibition of horse training di-
rected by the world's first horseman in the art of dressage and haute école, Captain Philip de Pluminel, for-
merly with the Cadre Noir of the French Cavalry School!"*

"Entrez," the captain whispered softly to the mare.
She went forward while he remained behind the curtain, his face showing no trace of nervousness or even
excitement. He was a man in full command of himself
and the horse in the ring.

Into the complete darkness and the silence came the first sounds of the music. It was faint, almost impossible to hear, and then it swelled, flowing throughout the hall. The captain could sense the rise in tension as the people waited for something to happen. They were under the spell of darkness and expectation.

He knew that few among them realized that his music had been composed to create just that feeling—that *anything* might happen. It faded away again to the faintest of sounds and, finally, stopped as abruptly as it had begun.

The captain smiled in the darkness. The audience was still silent, but he knew that they were growing apprehensive. They must be straining their eyes and ears for the faintest sound or movement from the ring.

Once again the music came, this time with a dreamlike slowness as if carried on a summer wind, and barely audible. It echoed through the hall, percussive but muted with a thin, haunting piping sound. Then the rhythm became brisk, followed by a long flute passage, a new movement, as gentle as rain, the soft sounds stealing through the hall, mysterious, remote, and ever-haunting.

Suddenly the spotlight came on to bathe the mare standing quietly, peacefully, in the center of the ring. Her head was lowered, as if she were grazing in pasture rather than standing in the tanbark of a circus ring. She would remain that way until her next musical cue; a shrill piping note, constantly repeated.

The captain's eyes never left her silver-gray body. A moment went by while the mare remained ghostly still, as if under the deep spell of the music. The sounds carried far, the notes seeming to stretch out infinitely. It was weird, uncanny music, to him who had created it as well as to the audience. He listened to the receding echoes and could almost hear the cries of distant birds. It was ominous music and yet with it came a sort of joy, an excitement, an intoxicating sense of danger.

He heard the first of the piping notes faintly in the background. It was the signal for his mare to begin. He watched her lift her small head and gaze into the darkness outside the ring. She seemed startled. Her tension mounted as the notes were repeated and became louder.

She turned her head as if she didn't know where the sounds were coming from or why. She began trotting around the ring, slowly at first, but as the notes quickened so did her flying feet. The notes became a horrible whistling. She slowed abruptly, as if realizing there was no running away from the crackling noise. The notes became slow with her strides, even sly, with long pauses in between.

She continued trotting around the ring but now her strides kept time with the notes. She paused with each syncopated step, dancing as she moved in measured, cadenced strides, the embodiment of supreme grace and beauty.

The captain missed nothing as he watched her floating about the ring with no movement of ears or nostrils. Like a ghost, he thought, her namesake—but a ghost only in her lightness of foot. She was very much alive, his mare. Everything in her was attuned to the music. She raised her legs high in time to the rhythm.

The pauses between the shrill notes became longer. Obediently, she slowed her strides without lessening their lofty height, giving the impression of barely touching the ground as she moved forward.

He watched her perform the *passage,* and wondered how anyone in the audience could not be captivated by her dancing fire, even if ignorant of the noble art of dressage in its highest form. There was no evidence of her great strength being tried in the disciplined, controlled trot. Instead, it was as if she performed that slow measured pace for her own delight.

Did the Swedes appreciate what she was doing riderless? he wondered. Without benefit of physical commands of hands and legs to prompt and guide her into the movements of *haute école?* Almost every circus could boast of having a horse and rider skilled in dressage. But no horse, so far as he knew, could give such an exhibition alone! It had taken years of hard work to achieve this perfection!

The music grew louder, flowing around him and into the hall. The piping notes in the background were barely audible but he heard them, as she did. They became more distinct, more commanding, and her movements changed quickly.

She slowed her forward movement still more without the slightest change in gait or lofty carriage. Suddenly she was trotting in place, her hoofs faultless in their timing, and dancing like the "god-horse" the ringmaster had announced. Truly, she did not look earth-bound!

The captain watched her perform the *piaffe* with critical eyes, and saw no mistakes. In all the years they had worked together, she had never been as faultless as now.

Finally the music stopped and she was released from the *piaffe*. She made a slow circuit of the ring, then stopped to stand magnificently in the spotlight as if awaiting the acclaim she knew she deserved.

With great effort, the captain controlled his anger at the crowd's polite but restrained applause. In every other country they had played she had received a tumul-tuous ovation at this moment. His disappointment was not for himself but for her. He knew she missed the cheering. Always, she reacted to a stirring wave of applause by working better.

As if in a great cathedral, the crowd waited without word or sound for the mare to go into her next display. The captain resented the coldness of the elegantly dressed audience. Were the Swedes unimaginative as well as dull and unappreciative? Were their reactions based on what they knew was expected of them as a nation of reserved and practical people?

He was angry inside and he sought to quell the mounting hot temperament of his own blood. Yet a freezing coldness was there too, controlled but with an ever-creeping deadliness. He concealed it well. Nothing showed in his face. He looked calm and dispassionate, his eyes a steady, black stare.

He watched his mare as she quickly responded to the

clash of cymbals by breaking into a canter. The cadence of her hoofs picked up as if she had been eagerly awaiting the change of pace. And yet her quickening strides were more floating than driving, so she appeared no more earthbound than she had at a trot.

Faster and faster she circled the ring until she was in a gallop. Suddenly she spun on her hind legs, pirouetting in place and spinning in a small circle as if she sought to drive a hole into the tanbark with her hoofs.

The music rose to a great crescendo and a moment later she lifted her forelegs in the air at an acute angle while balancing herself on her hind legs. She held this pose for several seconds before coming down.

The captain waited for the crowd to applaud her *levade,* and when the rippling of applause finally came he smiled. She was reaching them and she had much more to give.

To the roll of the drums, she rose again in the *levade* and finished with four jumps on her hind legs that carried her across the ring in the *courbette.* Only then did she bring down her forelegs and trot slowly around the ring, still swaying to the music, forever dancing.

His heart went out to her, for he knew how much she enjoyed her dancing. It was the woman in her, he thought. No stallion, no gelding he had ever trained could equal her lightness of foot, her natural rhythm.

He no longer cared if the crowd applauded or not. It made little difference now. He was celebrating with her these difficult movements brought to perfection by their many years of work together. Her own will had merged with his. She was indeed one with him in all respects.

Now, nearing the end of her performance, she was in the center of the ring. The music faded and only the shrill notes of the flute were heard. They became louder, as they had been at the beginning, and she responded quickly to these signals. Everything in her was alerted. It was evident in the movement of her muscles beneath the spotlight, in the quivering of her nostrils and the ceaseless twitching of her ears.

Once more the notes were so constant that they became a horrible whistle. As they approached their highest pitch, it appeared that she could no longer tolerate them and sought escape. She sprang into the air with her forelegs stretched out while drawing her hind legs beneath her in the difficult *ballotade*.

The captain was unmindful of the applause. He heard only the horrible whistling notes and his eyes were only for the mare. Again she rose from the ground. This time in midair she kicked out her hind legs savagely in unison with her forelegs as if to ward off a pursuer. Truly she appeared to be a winged horse, a Pegasus, soaring through the air, her head raised high and her mane and tail flying!

The breath-taking *capriole* was the climax of her performance and when she had finished the lights in the great hall went on, growing in brightness and brilliance. The mare stood still in the center of the ring, her ears alert, her nostrils flaring.

The ringmaster motioned the captain forward and he joined his mare reluctantly, standing beside her in his dark evening clothes.

He raised his hand to acknowledge the ever-mounting

applause of the crowd when they saw him. Like her, his movements were proud, cool and controlled. It was not as he had wanted it. They applauded now because he stood with her beneath glaring lights and they were able to see and judge the act for what it had been—a serious exhibition of horse training.

Few Swedes cared about imagination of any sort, he decided. They wanted their Art to be obedient and useful, nothing that might ever excel and surpass life itself. They had seen no ghost-horse, no winged Pegasus—only a well-trained animal. They would not waste their time pursuing idle fantasies. They had no part in his own imaginative world.

He had little use for such practical people, and he did not want to be influenced or changed by them and others of their kind. He ceased listening to the applause and concentrated only on his mare and his own thoughts. He stroked her neck beneath the gray mane.

This was to be his last circus performance in Europe for he had agreed to a contract with Ringling Bros. Barnum and Bailey in the United States. It meant a well-deserved vacation for him and his mare; they would not have to work again until he joined the Ringling Circus at its training quarters in Florida.

He would leave this land of coldness behind to pursue something he'd wanted to do all his life. He would visit Haiti on his way to the United States and find out for himself what the land of his ancestors was truly like. He had heard many strange things about Haiti and a legend that was filled with impossible events—one he'd been told by his father, when a child, passed on from generation to generation as part of their heritage. He had an overpowering urge to learn more about the legend and, because he believed in signs and omens, the contract with Ringling Bros. coming at this time pointed the way.

The applause continued and he saw some children standing up and hanging over a balcony rail, waving their programs at him. He waved back, knowing they had seen *The Ghost* as he had planned they should see her. The circus was for children and the imagination of children.

The lights dimmed except for the yellow spotlight as he backed his beloved mare out of the ring. Little did she know what he had in store for her across the ocean. He wanted her to have a foal and he had found the stallion that was right for her in every way. He had seen him on Swedish television only that week, a horse called the Black, the American champion, winning a great race in Florida. That he should find such a stallion now, after so many years of searching, was still another sign that pointed the way for him. He was determined that nothing would keep him from acquiring the Black for his mare. He was a man who took what he wanted. He was as remorseless as he was powerful.

The applause continued long after he stepped behind the black velvet curtain, but he did not return to acknowledge it.

2 · *The Black Stallion*

The stallion tossed his head, sniffing the spring air with dilated nostrils. He was a coal-black silhouette against the golden light of early morning. Within his great body was a fierce, insistent, almost intolerable longing for a mate. He became more excited than ever when the wind brought the sharp odor of mares to him from a distant pasture.

He gave a sudden shrill neigh which was clearly meant for the mares he could not see but knew were there. He gathered himself, rocked back on his hindquarters, and plunged forward. The morning echoed to the wild pounding of his hoofs as he raced down the field, his black

15

mane and long thick tail gleaming brilliantly in the sun.

He kept close to the arrow-straight fence which separated him from other paddocks and fields like his own, all green with lush grass. When he came to the end he stretched his head high, peering over the top board.

Now he could see the mares and he shrilled again the high clear note of the stallion—challenging and passionate and urgent with life. His calls shattered the morning stillness and some of the mares raised their heads and turned his way. A few began to gallop in wide circles but the majority continued grazing as if they had not heard his love call. He repeated his clear happy neigh of desire, hoping to attract the running mares— but soon they too turned away from him and continued grazing.

In ever-mounting fury and frustration he raced back and forth along the high fence, displaying all his speed and strength and fire. When he stopped it was only to paw the ground and send clods of earth flying. His neigh changed with his stomping; it became more metallic and threatening, more demanding than loving.

The mares raised their heads again and listened. They saw the stallion in all his maturity and masterfulness. They listened to his calls which rang so defiantly across the field. Then, as one, they took flight, streaming away from him in a tangle of bodies and plunging hoofs.

He watched them go, his eyes sparkling with a savage fire. He continued snorting and the veins beneath his silken coat swelled. He rushed madly in a wild gallop that sent the earth flying from his hoofs.

Later, when his anger was spent, he sought the shade

of a towering oak tree. There he carefully lowered his body to the ground. He rolled over, his legs hanging limply in the air, and rubbed his back and hindquarters against the cool turf.

Alec Ramsay had watched his horse from a perch on the top board of the fence. "Is that the way to behave?" he called to the Black. "You should know better."

The stallion continued rolling, paying no attention to him. It didn't matter; Alec had learned long ago to speak to the Black whether or not the stallion listened.

Alec smelled the pungent odor of steaming cane juice in the air and looked beyond the green carpet of fenced pastures to the tall chimneys of a distant sugar mill. Long columns of gray smoke floated and wavered above the stacks, scenting the land with an almost overpowering sweetness. Sugarfoot Ranch was an appropriate name for this place, he decided.

After having spent the previous two months in the teeming coastal city of Miami, Alec had not expected south-central Florida to be as enjoyable as it was. Most winter visitors, like himself, were lured to the coastal areas and never saw the vast, sparsely populated region on the edge of the Everglades.

He turned his face to the tropical sun, enjoying it and the peaceful quiet. His hard body beneath T-shirt and Levis was as brown as his face. He was thoroughly happy with his well-earned vacation after the grueling races at Hialeah Park in Miami. There was no one around to tell him what to do. The Black was his sole responsibility. It was almost as it had been in the beginning, so long ago.

He watched a great heron in long-legged flight against the blue sky and listened to its raucous cry. He followed it as it flew low over a grove of tall cocoanut palms, the fronds moving languidly in the soft breeze.

His gaze returned to his horse and he found the Black still lying on his back, his hind legs drawn up and forelegs spread outward. He smiled; it was a most unusual position for a horse who led such an active life. Perhaps the Black too was succumbing to the languor of this land.

Alec shifted his body in order to get into a more comfortable position on the fence. He wondered if this might not be an ideal place to raise horses. Henry Dailey had suggested as much before leaving to oversee the training of several two-year-olds in New York. Henry, his old friend and trainer, had suggested they might even purchase a small farm in this area as an annex to Hopeful Farm up north. They would move their young stock here and, perhaps, some of the older horses that needed a long rest in the sun.

It was not a new idea, Alec had reminded Henry, for the Ocala area in upper central Florida had become very popular with horse breeders as a year-round operation.

"Too popular," Henry had answered. "Land is more costly there, and we don't need to be with the others. This area is worth considering. Think about it while I'm gone."

There were advantages and disadvantages to it, Alec thought. The area was more suitable for the growing of sugar cane and vegetables than pasture grass. It was reclaimed swampland, the soil a black carpet of peat muck. Beneath it, of course, was the solid bedrock of coral limestone that shaped and held the Florida peninsula.

The rich farmland had been reclaimed by a flood control basin which the United States Army Engineers had constructed to contain the waters of Lake Okeechobee to the north. They had diverted the waters which normally had flowed over this area and drifted south to nourish the Everglades. It had meant thousands of square miles of new agricultural land and communities. But it also meant, Alec reflected bitterly, the ultimate death of the great swamp. More and more canals were being built, not only by the Army engineers but by private developers, promising "residential neighborhoods where wild animals once lived."

Alec turned and faced south, where he could see an endless tawny blaze of light that seemed to merge and mingle with the rays of the rising sun. He was at the doorstep of the wild Everglades, and after what he had read and heard of the immensity of the swamp he wondered if bulldozers and draglines would ever be able to transform it completely into the realtors' promised Garden of Eden. He stared in that direction a long time.

Finally he roused himself, shaking his head and wondering why on this morning he should be drawn to the swamp, as if by a magnet, when he never had thought much about it before.

Perhaps, he decided, the peace, the languor or whatever one wished to call it was changing his metabolism as it seemed to be doing to the Black this very moment. He jumped down from the fence, determined to disturb the quiet of the morning. He rode the Black daily and today must be no exception. The spring racing season would open soon in New York and they were scheduled to be there. Henry had given them a few weeks to freshen up from their hard winter campaign but no more than that.

He walked over to his horse, wondering if he'd be able to acquire another paddock for him. It was the first time he'd seen mares turned out in the adjacent field, and he did not want the Black distracted. It was difficult enough in the spring of the year without having a band of broodmares in the next field! He knew that mares generally coped with the breeding season better than stallions; they possessed female patience whereas stallions, once started on a breeding program, felt only the persistent drive to mate.

He was glad Henry had not been around to see the mares in the adjacent pasture. He'd have raised the devil. It was an oversight, Alec knew, and he'd be able to straighten it out with Joe Early, the ranch manager, later in the day.

The Black had rolled over on his side and was the picture of a horse completely at ease. His eyes were open and when he saw Alec coming toward him with the lead shank he scrambled to his feet. He did not run away but stood still—as quiet as the morning—proud and long-limbed, waiting.

Alec snapped the shank on the halter ring. He never got tired of looking at his horse. He would always stand in awe of the Black, no matter how long he had him.

Few ever saw the true greatness in the Black without

standing close to him. No picture could convey it. Nor could it be seen from fence rail or grandstand, as electric as his presence and speed might be. One had to stand beside him to appreciate the arrogance and nobility that were stamped on his small fine head. One had to rub him with soft cloths and brushes to see how well every part of his seventeen-hand body fitted together to make him the greatest runner of all time.

Alec watched the stallion's ears, for his horse talked with his ears. Now they flicked south in the direction of the Everglades.

Alec answered with his hands, running them down the arched neck. Then he said aloud, "You too? Okay, we'll go that way this morning if only for a change of scenery."

His fingers rubbed the ridge of the stallion's neck. "We're on vacation, you and I," he said. "We can do pretty much as we please with Henry gone."

There was a long sun-filled day ahead of them. Early up and early to bed, that alone was the rule on vacation and an easy one to keep.

"You're a good fellow," Alec said softly. The Black turned his head toward him, as if listening attentively. Alec knew that his horse understood the warmth of his words if not the precise meaning, and that was all that mattered. He felt the stallion's breath against his face. There was a gentleness, too, about his horse which few people ever saw. The large eyes gazed calmly and trustfully into his own.

"We'd probably get pretty lazy staying here all the time," he said. "You and I need a change of seasons. I don't think this place would be good for us at all."

The Black snorted.

"Not that we can't have fun here," Alec continued, rubbing the soft muzzle. "And there's no reason why we can't see some of the swamp today. No reason at all."

He paused before mounting, aware of an odd feeling coming over him. It was vague but there, an awareness that this morning somehow was not like other mornings. He shrugged his shoulders. Today was like any other day, he told himself, except that he would ride south for a change and do some exploring.

He passed a hand along the stallion's backbone, waiting for the headiness, almost a feeling of momentary intoxication, to leave him. He decided that the feeling might be one of pure joy at having his horse to himself for a change.

It had taken three days of Henry's absence for him to realize how glad he was to be free of the trainer's yoke. He longed for complete abandon and freedom of movement, if only for a short while. Ahead of him was a long summer of racing, unremitting in its toil and preparation. And, when he wasn't racing, there was work to be done at Hopeful Farm. Good help was hard to get and even more difficult to keep. Every free day would be used to help repair fences and barns, to harrow paddocks, to care for the new foals and to cut, bale and store hay for the winter. One never caught up. Time taken out—even for racing—was never regained.

Alec thought longingly of the days when his every move did not have to be obedient and useful, when he could be off on the Black, to go where he liked and as he pleased.

"Why not ride bareback this morning?" he asked himself. "Why not leave the saddle and bridle behind? Why not ride him the way I used to?"

Alec reached up and grasped the stallion's mane with both hands. He spoke to the Black as he backed up beside the horse's head. Then he took two short springy steps forward and swung his legs up while pulling on the mane at the same time. His body rolled and twisted in the air, reaching for seventeen hands of horse!

He landed astride the Black, his hands and legs communicating immediately to his horse in a language of their own. He could control the Black's direction and pace by the pressure of a knee or calf, by the touch of a heel on his flank or a hand on his neck. Sometimes all that was necessary was a sound from his lips.

There would be no bridle or saddle today—no restrictions upon him or his horse. This *was* going to be a different kind of a day!

He squeezed his horse into a canter and cued him into a left lead. He made a large circle, hastening and smoothing the stallion's strides until he had him almost in a full gallop.

"Too fast, too cocky," he warned himself, slowing down the Black as they approached the closed gate of the paddock.

When they were outside, Alec turned the Black south and did not check his horse's speed. He was happier than he'd been in a long time. He was not merely at home on the Black; he belonged entirely to him. It was as if he had no other existence. There was no room for anything else.

The stallion's strides came swift and easy, between a gallop and a run, what race-track people call a "breeze." Alec settled down to enjoy the ride. In a short while he'd slow down the Black but for the moment he let the wind water his eyes. He listened to the beat of the Black's hoofs over the dirt road. The secret of his horse's success lay not only in his great strength and speed but also in his perfect rhythm and unwasted motion.

Alec moved closer to the stallion's neck and adjusted himself to the rhythm of the stallion's strides. He felt a sudden urge to let him go into a headlong run, for the sound of the Black's running hoofs had always broken the world apart for him! The taste of the wind, when the Black was in full flight, brought him greater joy than anything else in the world!

Alec spoke softly, a sound rather than a word, and the Black broke swiftly into full run. The triple, throbbing beat of his racing hoofs over the dirt road came faster and louder. He thrust out his small head as if ready to extend himself to the fullest; his haunches glittered in the early morning sun like black satin.

Alec's eyes were as bright as his mount's. The Black was reveling in his freedom from bit and saddle! Still, Alec knew he must keep him under control. He pushed away the stallion's mane that streamed back at him, clearing his blurred eyes so he could see objects along the road. Instinctively he began estimating furlongs and began counting off the seconds, down to fifths of seconds, keeping time in his mind. Every jockey needed to know the pace of his mount, whether running at full speed or not, and Alec never stopped practicing because he knew it was not a question of talent but hard work. Also, he didn't want the Black to run himself into the ground.

After a mile, he slowed the Black to a walk. He let go of the mane and wiped the sweat from his face. They were close enough to the Everglades for him to be able to smell the rank odor that blew from the swamp.

Suddenly the air took on a warning bite. Alec had the same feeling he'd had earlier, an awareness that this morning was not like other mornings. Only now another element had been added. He stopped the Black in his tracks. He didn't know if the *danger* he felt was real or something he sensed in the air around him. But he knew it was there, somewhere in the Everglades.

3 · The Hammocks

Alec's gaze swept over the saw-grass empire, colored like ripe wheat nearby but shading to emerald green in the distance. It was a wild bright plain, neither land nor water, with no visible limits. It was a land older than time, most of it untouched by human hands. It was motionless—and yet Alec sensed in it a throbbing heartbeat of its own.

He shrugged off the feeling of apprehension that had come to him. There was no reason to fear this watery wilderness that was being drained by the canals. He realized that the huge swamp was resisting, fighting for its life. This was evident in the sun-bitten vastness spreading before him as if in challenge to all those who sought to destroy it.

The dirt road went to a remote and isolated Seminole Indian village a couple of miles away. The people there were hunters, he had been told, and lived on one of the high islands in the swamp known as hammocks.

His gaze turned to the nearest hammock, a round clump of land with tall palms silhouetted against the brazen sky. There were some birds flying above it and he watched them vanish behind the palm fronds. There were other hammocks to the west, some larger, others smaller, all emerging from the green-and-yellow-speared sea.

Alec moved his horse on. He had come this far, and there was no reason to turn back now. He did not mind the quiet of the swamp after the months of pandemonium at Hialeah race track.

Just ahead, a score of buzzards rose from a mud flat at the sound of the Black's hoofs. Alec watched them move awkwardly in swift-waddling flight. They didn't go far but stayed directly above, planing in lazy circles, waiting for him to pass.

When he rode by he saw a dead alligator, its body furnishing forage for the hideous carrion birds. The buzzards had ripped flesh and entrails into a shredded horror; he turned away.

For the first time Alec thought of the devastation to wildlife that the drainage canals must even now be bringing to the Everglades. Yet, as he looked at the immensity of the land that stretched as far south as the Gulf of Mexico, he doubted that the swamp ever would be conquered completely by man. It was not meant for human habitation. It belonged to wildlife alone.

Later he came to an unexpected fork in the road and brought the Black to a halt. One way led to the Seminole Indian village while the other road wound its way through the vast wilderness of swamp to the southwest. Far in the distance Alec saw a large hammock and decided the road went there. Perhaps it was one used as a base by hunters.

He would go in that direction rather than to the Indian village. The road had been built high, creating a dike that held surface water within the area. The sawgrass spears were tall and green beyond, and he would have a chance to see part of the true swamp before draglines and bulldozers destroyed it.

Alec kept the Black at a slow canter, knowing he could go to the distant hammock and back without ever tiring his horse. The stallion's ears were alert; he would miss nothing and appeared as eager as Alec to go on.

For several miles, he rode in a silence that seemed to become part of his bloodstream. The hot sun beat down mercilessly on his bare head and he felt as if he were crossing a desert and looking forward to reaching an oasis in the distant hammock. A dusty brown snake crossed the road just ahead and disappeared into the saw grass. It might be a water moccasin, he thought, and cautioned himself that he must not let the heat and silence dull his senses.

For a long while he rode on until, finally, he approached the hammock. It was even larger than he'd thought and the trees created a towering wall of cypress before him, making it difficult to tell where land left off and the dark water of the swamp began. The water rose high around the cypress knees and the hammock appeared all the more ghostly with Spanish moss hanging from the trees in heavy shrouds. There was a graveyard hush to the stillness and, for the first time, Alec thought seriously of turning back.

The road seemed to ring the hammock and he saw a colorful array of air plants and orchids within the green gloom. Despite the ominous hush, the natural beauty of the hammock attracted him. He decided to go a little farther.

The road finally turned onto the hammock, disappearing into a stand of tall yuccas. Alec followed it, glad to leave the merciless glare of the sun behind if only for a short while.

The road narrowed to barely more than a white shell path curling around the western end of the hammock. It skirted the silent stand of cypress trees and the dark water in which they grew, then turned away from the moist bank to wind its way through the hammock.

He never had seen a more beautiful natural park, made all the more impressive by the saw-grass wasteland behind him. It was indeed a startling contrast and his eyes swept to the magnificent stands of cocoanut palms and live oaks, the beautiful magnolias and oleanders.

He heard the first sound of life in the dense foliage, a slight whirring noise. The Black heard it too; his ears were pitched in the direction of a patch of wild grape-

vine. A moment later Alec saw a hummingbird forag-
ing among the vines, its wings whirring like a helicopter
propeller as it hovered about a flower.

He continued riding down the shell path, his imagination beginning to run wild. Where did the path lead
and what would he find? He knew he would be warned
of any danger by the Black's animal instinct. As it was,
his horse was moving easily, almost as if he too wanted
to find out where the path led.

Through a screen of moss-laden oak trees they emerged
into a small clearing. It had been hacked from the jungle
growth, probably by Indians many years ago, and kept
clear by the occasional hunter who used the hammock.

There was a rough hollow in the center of the clearing, and the Black moved toward it of his own accord.
He lowered his head, his nostrils sniffing the ground.
When he straightened, he gave vent to a clear, happy
neigh of desire!

Shocked by the Black's soft call, Alec slipped off his
back and studied the impressions in the dirt. What he
found brought him quickly back to time and place. A
horse had rolled in the hollow not long before and,
judging from the Black's neigh, it had been a mare!

The shell path led into the jungle on the opposite side
of the clearing, and Alec knew he had to follow it. He
could not turn back without knowing why another horse
and rider were there. For certainly the mare was not
alone.

"You be quiet and we'll see what goes," he said.

Alec had led the Black only a short distance when he
came to an abrupt stop, startled by a peculiar kind of

whistle. It was a piping note, constantly repeated. It came from one place, then another, with low, sly pauses in between.

There was a crackling noise from a nearby hedge and Alec's eyes swept toward it. He saw nothing.

For a moment the notes ended and the profound silence was almost as unnerving as the sounds had been. Alec felt the heavy, oppressive heat of the day. Not a leaf stirred in the creeping jungle growth. He heard no whisper of life. The very stillness of the air held him as if by some strange magic while sweet and heavy odors filled his nostrils.

The peculiar notes had come from some kind of bird he did not know, he decided. This land and its inhabitants were completely foreign to him.

He moved down the path again, although there was barely room to lead the Black. The ferns grew thick and green on either side and the trees shut out the sun, leaving them more in dusk than day.

The silence was broken by the bird once more. At least, Alec believed it was a bird. There was no other explanation for the sound. It seemed to be following him. He mustn't think of it as anything else. The piping notes were making him more and more uncomfortable. Now he wasn't at all certain they came from a bird. They were too high, too piercing, too demanding. *Where were they coming from and why?*

He brought the Black to a stop. All he had to do was turn back. Yet he was reluctant to do so. He wanted to find out where the path led and what another horse and rider were doing there.

The notes ended and there was nothing but the great silence again. Alec couldn't analyze the way he felt. He would have liked to believe it was all nonsense but it wasn't. There was something about the notes, something he didn't understand but that might be made clear if he went on. He moved the Black forward.

Once he thought he saw something gliding overhead, high in the trees and obscured by the heavy Spanish moss. It appeared to be white—perhaps a broad-winged wood ibis nesting in the trees—but he couldn't be sure in the misty, shimmering heat. At any rate, he heard no more notes and was glad of it.

The path ended at a narrow channel of dark water. The opposite side of the stream had been cleared of wild reeds and in the muck Alec saw the prints of a man and a horse!

There was no turning back now, he knew. The winding dark water was like a slithering snake but it was shallow enough to ford without swimming. There was no sign of any alligators and it would take only a few seconds to cross.

There was no need to coax the Black into the water. He went forward, wading with Alec through the shallows. He was eager to keep going but Alec brought him to a stop on the other side and placed a gentle hand upon the stallion's nose. Alec's instincts told him that he must proceed with the utmost caution. There was no reason to fear the presence of another horse and rider but until he found out what they were doing there it was best to be careful.

The path became increasingly difficult, leading through

twisting vines that only recently had been cut to clear the way. On either side was a forbidding fortress of winding tendrils, wrapped about tree trunks and locked in a continuous mesh that defied all but the sharpest machetes. Even now the vines had begun the work of re-closing the gap across the shell path.

Alec felt uneasy at the jungle net closing in on him. He told himself that he could turn back any time he wanted, that he did not have to go farther if he felt it was not worth the risk.

The upper branches of huge trees and the thick shrouds of Spanish moss hid the sun, leaving him in a world of dusk. But despite his apprehension, he was determined to go on. How long ago had he left the farm? Only this morning? His contact with it seemed to have faded away.

It was as if he were living in another world, one as timeless as the swamp itself. He felt out of place, and yet for a reason he could not understand, much less explain, a strong motivation compelled him to complete what had become an urgent mission. It drove him onward.

Finally the shell path came to an abrupt end. But it was not the end of his journey. The vines in the area had been cut away completely and there was sufficient room between the trees for him to continue. He led the Black forward.

A few minutes later he came in sight of a large clearing. Actually it was a meadow carpeted with cropped grass, a slab of green on the edge of the endless swamp. He heard the splash of a bird in the distant water, then the scream of an osprey as it rose above the saw grass. It was a mysterious cry in the vast void of emptiness. Alec paused a moment beside the huge trunk of an oak tree.

At the far end of the meadow he saw the gleam of a silver body and heard the soft beat of hoofs. Cautiously he moved in that direction, aware that his excitement matched that of the stallion at his side.

When he reached the edge of the clearing he saw a tall black man riding a gray mare.

4 · The Captain

Alec clamped a hand across his horse's nostrils, stilling the neigh that was about to come. "No," he said softly.

His eyes followed the man riding the gray mare. He wore the clothes of a southern farm laborer—sunbleached trousers and a gray cotton shirt. On his head was a wide-rimmed straw hat, his thick hair falling below it and as blue-black as an Indian's. But despite his appearance, the man failed completely to look the part of a farm laborer.

No one but a professional horseman could sit in the saddle as this man did. He was still and unmoving while his mare trotted with the most airy steps, gliding across the grass, turning as if magically summoned one way and then another.

Alec knew the man must be guiding her but there was no obvious movement of his hands or legs. He used no stirrups or spurs; his calves and thighs were directing his horse.

Alec's heart was racing now. The mare was as light-footed as a ghost and, in fact, *if she had been a ghost* he would not have been more astonished by what he saw! Here, deep in the Everglades, he was watching the disciplined movement of *haute école!* He had never before seen a horse schooled in these movements perform in the United States. Only in Europe—at the Spanish Riding School in Vienna, Austria—had he watched the famed Lipizzan stallions in this advanced art of training and horsemanship.

This was no Lipizzan but a horse of many strains, including Arabian; yet she performed the dancing steps as well as any horse Alec had seen in Austria. If the man riding her knew he was being watched he gave no indication of it. He sat like a statue in the saddle, his black face cold and masklike. He moved her in a wider circle, coming closer to Alec. His guiding movements were still not visible and yet the cadence of the mare's hoofs picked up as if she had been eagerly awaiting the change of pace. Suddenly she was spinning around on her hind legs, pirouetting in place.

The man was part of his horse as she moved at full speed while fixed to one spot. Alec realized that many years of intensive training must have been spent on the mare for her to perform this difficult movement.

Finally the mare came out of the pirouettes and made a slow circle. It was only then that Alec saw her rider's first movement, although it had nothing to do with cues to his horse. He raised a hand to pull his straw hat more firmly down on his head so as not to lose it.

Alec ignored the man's wide-rimmed hat as he did the laborer's clothes. One who knew the art of high school riding and training as this man did would not make his living working in the cane fields!

The mare swept diagonally across the circle, shoulder in, then shoulder out coming back, her hoofs skimming effortlessly over the grass.

Alec knew she was being subjected to the light pressures of her rider's hands and legs. Every nerve in her was awaiting the next signal from him.

Alec forgot where he was, forgot everything but the fact that for the first time in his life he was witnessing a supreme exhibition of horsemanship. Never had he seen such unity of horse and rider!

Spellbound, he watched the mare move across the ground in flowing turns and glides and figurations he had never seen before, all in a strangely wonderful dance made even more magical by the ghostly silence of the Everglades.

Then the tempo of her hoofs increased and Alec knew the exhibition was coming to an end. She made a high leap, her hind and forelegs stretched out so that she looked as if she were truly flying! When she came down, she rocked back and forth on her hindquarters before rising in a *levade* of supreme grace, staying up longer than Alec had ever thought possible, her neck arched while she reached for the sky with her forequarters. She came down slowly and stood still.

The black stallion's clear, high neigh rang through the stillness of the hammock too quickly for Alec to stop it. The silver-gray mare turned her ears in his direction and answered. But her rider did not so much as glance toward the intruders.

The Black pawed the ground and neighed again. Alec did not try to quiet him, for his eyes were on the rider. The man had turned in their direction; slowly, he doffed his wide-rimmed hat.

"Hello!" he called. His voice was oddly deep with a strong French accent.

Alec remained where he was, mindful again of Henry's final instructions. *"Above anything else keep him away from mares."*

He watched the man come forward as if riding on air rather than a horse. His shoulders were immense and his head was held high in an arrogant manner. He must be over six feet tall, Alec decided, for his legs were as long and powerful as his arms. His body was heavy yet lithe, bulky yet smoothly muscled and carrying not an ounce of superfluous fat. He looked every bit the professional horseman he was, not the farm laborer the clothes represented. Why was he dressed as he was? What was he doing there?

Alec's grip tightened on the Black's halter. He saw at least a week's growth of beard on the stern face. The eyes were inquisitive, as well they should be at finding someone watching his performance. But there was also a coldness in them that foreboded danger. There was no getting away now. He had to face up to this meeting.

Alec allowed his gaze to shift to the mare, noting the lightness of the narrow reins and bridle. Then he looked at the man and said, "I enjoyed watching you very much. I've never seen a performance quite like it."

"It's centuries old," the man answered quietly. "You've wasted a great deal of time."

Alec's brows knit in puzzlement at the man's words. He searched for an explanation in the cold face, with its blunt nose, wide and high cheekbones, but found nothing. The man's eyes were only for the Black.

Suddenly the stallion bolted, trying to reach the mare. Alec managed to stop him but not before there was a hard impact of bodies. He pulled the Black away, talking to him all the while.

Anger glittered in the man's eyes and it was evident that the mare felt his annoyance. Her body moved violently. There was a gentle pressure of the man's hands and it was enough to restrain her.

"I'm sorry about that," Alec said.

"It was to be expected." The man's gaze remained on the stallion. "It is good to hear one talk to animals as you do," he added. "It is a simple thing but few seem to know it is the only way."

Alec was used to having professionals scrutinize his horse, just as he too carefully noted everything about another's. He studied the mare before him. She possessed the full, unsloped croup and high-set tail so characteristic of the Arabian. Her long arched neck and slim sinewy legs indicated the desert breed as well. But her head, although tapered, did not have the dish-faced profile of the Arabian. And she had a slight ramlike convex nose common to Spanish-Barbary stock. She was broad of chest and deep through the heart like the Lipizzan, and had that breed's wider hips and back ribs. The additional "room inside" and the compactness of body structure gave her stamina as well as force.

Alec decided that she might well possess the best of many breeds—or, at least, the best for the kind of work she was doing. Her height was just under sixteen hands, and her weight was proportionate to her size, solid but not heavy. She was a mare he would have liked to own.

His gaze and thoughts returned to her rider as the man dismounted. Alec's first reaction was that he had been right—the man was well over six feet tall.

"My name is Captain Philip de Pluminel," he said.

Alec took the man's offered hand. "Mine is Alec Ramsay." He smiled, hoping the captain would smile back and, perhaps, explain what he was doing with such a highly trained horse on a remote hammock in the Everglades.

No smile appeared on the man's masklike face. Yet Alec found that it did not frighten him any longer. He recalled other horsemen who allowed no emotion to show on their faces so as to reveal nothing of themselves or their motives. Alec decided that he would let the captain divulge as much or as little as he chose without any prodding from him. If he read the dark face correctly, this was a man of experience, used to command

and, most of all, impatient with anyone who questioned him too closely. And, apparently, Alec's name meant nothing to the captain—just as the name Captain Philip de Pluminel was not familiar to him.

The mare became excited again, tossing her head and blowing through large dilated nostrils. The captain quieted her while keeping his eyes on the stallion.

"Your horse, *Monsieur* Ramsay," he said finally, "is superb. I have seen him before but only on the television. It was while I was in Sweden last month." Then his unblinking black eyes turned to Alec. "And you . . . yes, you were riding him in the race I saw. But I did not think . . ." He paused, his eyes revealing an emotion for the first time.

Alec was used to people looking surprised when they first met him. He was no one's idea of a prosperous and well-known rider. For one thing, he appeared too young, although most times he didn't feel it. And today he was wearing the most tattered jeans and worn-out boots he possessed. But the captain's bewildered look made him feel better about being there. The man was human after all.

"I apologize," the captain said, smiling for the first time. "I should have known right away, seeing you with such a horse."

"Not at all. You didn't expect to see me, any more than I did you." Alec paused and found it easier to meet the man's eyes. It was time for a question of his own. "And you . . . do you live here?"

There was no hesitation in the captain's reply; it was as if the barrier between them had been dropped quickly.

The smile remained on his thick lips as he said, "Only for a short time. My home is in France, but then . . ." He shrugged his shoulders. ". . . anywhere the circus plays I call home. I have a contract with your Ringling Bros. Barnum and Bailey Circus beginning in April."

Everything was falling in place. The winter training quarters of the Ringling Circus was in Venice, Florida, not far to the north. The captain and his mare were probably on their way to it, whatever his reason might be for stopping off at this remote hammock. Perhaps the captain's reason was little different from his own—an opportunity to "freshen up" in a place where no one knew him, preparing himself and his mare for the hard season to come. If he looked at it that way, Alec summed up, their meeting in the swamp was not frightening at all.

The Black pushed his body hard against him, and Alec knew he should get him out of there immediately. "I'd better go," he said, his gaze turning to his horse.

"There will be no trouble. We can keep them apart." The captain's words were clipped and more heavily accented than before in what seemed to be sudden urgency. "I would like you to stay very much." There was a long pause while Alec turned to him. "Please, *Monsieur* Ramsay, I beg you to stay, if only to have lunch with me."

"Lunch?" Alec repeated, more to himself than to the man. It seemed incongruous that in the middle of a swamp he should be asked graciously to lunch as if he were back in town. He looked beyond the meadow but saw nothing except jungle-choked mangroves etched against the incredible blue of the sky.

"My house is just a short distance away," the captain said, "and you must be tired. It will do you and your horse good to rest before starting back. As I say, there will be no problem with our horses. We are professionals, are we not?"

The captain did not wait for an answer but moved along, leading his mare toward the mangroves. Alec hesitated, then followed quickly—almost as if the decision had been made for him and he'd had no choice. He was amused by his thoughts. His inquisitiveness had been aroused and he wanted to learn more about Captain Philip de Pluminel. No harm could come from having lunch with him. And, as the captain had so rightly said, both he and the Black could use a rest before starting back.

The captain walked with the same lightness he had shown in the saddle. He moved more like a cat than a man over six feet tall and so heavily muscled. He strode along a wide path through the mangroves without once looking back to see if Alec followed; it was as if he expected nothing but obedience to his wishes.

Alec kept a strong hold on the Black's halter. He did not find the man's conceit amusing but was determined to know more about him. He found that he was a little apprehensive but not afraid. *Fear* was something he had no thought of ever disclosing to this man. He too could conceal his emotions when necessary.

Alec's steps slowed as they emerged from the mangroves and he found himself in a cultivated garden of riotous colors. The brilliant red of poinsettia bushes was everywhere and there were rows and rows of hibiscus and poinciana plants.

If he had had any doubt the flowering paradise was the work of man, he had only to look beyond. Near the edge of the saw-grass swamp was a house, shaded and half-hidden by towering trees and shrubs. Alec followed the captain toward it.

It looked like a farmhouse and it had been built on stilts, perhaps to keep out the high water of the swamp during the rainy season. But as they drew closer, Alec saw it was like no farmhouse he'd ever seen before. The roof was fantastic. It rose high in the center and was topped by a strange-looking tower. What made it even more fantastic was that the roof dipped down on the opposite side almost to the ground! Never in his life had Alec ever seen a more ridiculous-looking building. It was made of unpainted cypress wood but looked more like one built of papier-mâché by a completely demented person.

Without a word, the captain strode onto a path that led toward the rear of the house, not bothering to glance behind to note Alec's reaction to the strange-looking house. He crossed another clearing and went directly to a small barn.

Alec waited while the captain put the mare away. The Black hated to see her go and there seemed to be no end to his nickering.

When the captain returned he said, "I have another

place for your horse." His eyes were evasive and Alec felt the first stirring of fear within him. He shrugged it off and followed.

Beyond the barn and deep in a grove of cocoanut palms, they came to a low shed, freshly whitewashed. The captain pulled open the double doors. Inside was a single room with a dirt floor, empty of machinery and adequate for use as a temporary stall.

"He'll be all right here," the captain said. "We can give him water and a bit of hay."

Alec nodded. It would be only a short while before he'd be leaving.

After taking care of his horse, he walked alongside the captain toward the house. There was some kind of game going on between them, he decided; it was apparent the captain wouldn't impart any information willingly and Alec was determined to wait him out.

They went up the long steps leading to the front entrance and Alec noted the strange symbols and ornaments carved on the heavy oaken door. The interior was dim for the few windows in it were shuttered and deeply recessed. As his eyes became adjusted to the semi-darkness, he saw a large living room with hand-hewn beams running across the ceiling and a great fireplace in which a fire was smoldering. The odor of burning wood filled the room.

It was a hot day and yet the house was chilly, even cold, despite the fire. Alec shivered. He couldn't be sure whether it was the cold or his mounting uneasiness that caused it.

The captain's tall figure moved across the room, momentarily blocking out the light from a window. He called loudly, *"Odin! Odin! Êtes-vous ici?"*

Alec's knowledge of French was only elementary but it was enough for him to understand that the captain had called, "Odin! Odin! Are you here?" Then the captain did not live alone. Who was Odin?

After a moment's hesitation, Alec followed the captain into the next room, which turned out to be the kitchen. It had a wood-burning stove, a large sink, a hand pump, and some utensils. But there was no one there and the captain left it for still another room beyond.

Alec went to the doorway and peered inside. The window shutters were closed and in the dim light of a kerosene lamp he could see an old man sitting on a high straight-backed chair. The captain stood beside him, speaking rapidly in French.

Alec made no attempt to understand what was being said. He was startled by the old man's appearance; he wore a big, shapeless black felt hat and in his right hand he held a long rod with a spear-tipped end.

Alec backed away from the doorway, then came to a stop as the old man rose from the chair and took a step toward him. Odin was wearing a crimson smock with some kind of gold braid around the edges. Beneath the smock Alec saw a laborer's corduroy trousers thrust into the tops of knee boots. The old man was gazing at him steadily and the captain, too, now turned in his direction.

Alec stood still, startled by the weird sight, his mind working feverishly. *Who were these people?* And this

Odin—his face was neither Indian nor Negro but a combination of both, and perhaps other races as well. His skin was old and weathered from decades of living in the sun, and yet his eyes were not aged at all. They burned into Alec's with almost savage intensity.

What had he walked into, so unprepared? he wondered.

The old man stood quietly, his legs astride, watching Alec. Then, suddenly, he raised a huge brown hand to his chest in some sort of ritualistic gesture. With that the captain spoke, as if on signal.

"I have explained to him that you are my guest," he said. "There is nothing to fear. He is just very old." The coldness in the captain's eyes made Alec feel uneasy despite the comforting words.

"But he is very capable despite his age," the captain continued. "He goes where he pleases and wants only to be left alone. Take his hand, Alec. I beg of you . . . *Je vous en prie*," he added urgently, his gaze returning to the old man.

Alec was frightened, feeling that anything might happen. He reached out for the old man's hand.

It felt cool and, despite its size and strength, there was no pressure at all. It was almost as if he were touching a ghost. Alec wondered if he was being successful in keeping the alarm from showing in his eyes.

They returned to the large living room, leaving the old man alone. The captain put his arm around Alec's shoulders and said warmly, "Now, we shall have our lunch and talk. We have much to discuss, *oui?*"

Alec looked at him. Those dark, unblinking eyes would

give nothing away. And Alec found that he didn't care about learning anything more. He wanted no answers to this mystery. His only thought now was to get away. He could no longer ignore the chill running down his spine and there was no way to stop it. The realization had come to him that there was not just *one* unstable man in this place, and of the two men the captain was the more dangerous.

5 · The Professionals

Alec realized that his sudden desire to leave came as no surprise to this man. He believed that the captain had expected it all along. He found the silence of the room and the man's cold stare more alarming than the fear within him.

Was the captain truly dangerous, as he believed, or were his suspicions brought about by this unusual house and the old man in the back room? Alec had never dreamed he could be so susceptible to moods and surroundings. It was as if his brain had become a battlefield of conflicting emotions.

The captain smiled at him, a small smile, almost a

grimace but a smile nevertheless. It threw Alec completely off balance again. There might not be anything to fear from this man, he told himself. The captain was eccentric, of course, a person of many moods, but not mad.

"It is not a cheerful house," the captain said quietly. "It was built more for shelter and protection than warmth and light. However, we can make it a little more pleasant."

He opened the large oak door, allowing the sun's rays to enter the room; then he opened the window shutters for still more light.

The captain's explanation and the brightness of the day helped rid Alec of some of his apprehensions. "Who is Odin?" he asked boldly.

"My great-uncle," the captain said quickly, as if he had anticipated the question. "He is a descendant of the Carib Indians, not the Seminoles. The Caribs were fierce warriors and knew this land long before the birth of Christ." He added nothing more, and Alec thought it wise to remain silent.

"Now for lunch," the captain said graciously. "If you'll excuse me a moment and make yourself at home . . ." He left the room, moving with the fluid grace of an animal.

Alec went over to the fireplace and sat down in one of the high-backed chairs. He was committed and there would be no leaving until after lunch. He looked around the room, noting the bareness of it. It didn't seem to have been occupied for very long; there were few personal things that made a house a home. A portable phonograph was on a table with several records beside it. It was battery-powered, for there was no electricity. Evidently the captain enjoyed music enough to carry a phonograph with him wherever he went.

A large kerosene lamp hung from the ceiling and there were several books on the table below it. Alec picked one up. It was on horsemanship and had been written by the captain himself. Since it was in French, Alec didn't attempt to read much of it but he was very impressed.

Had he allowed himself to give way to needless fears? Alec wondered. The captain was a professional horseman like himself and, according to the blurb on the jacket of the book, was the world's foremost authority on dressage.

Never in his life had Alec failed to get along with someone who loved horses. It was too strong a tie to be marred by his apprehensions, let alone *fear*. He had been ridiculous to believe otherwise, he told himself.

Another book Alec found on the table dealt with the Spanish conquest of Florida. It was for the serious student of history, being an English translation of Spanish documents written in the late 1560s. He noted penciled notations in French in the margins and wondered what they meant.

Alec put down the book, a little self-consciously, when the captain appeared carrying a wooden tray which he placed on the table. There were many kinds of canned meat as well as fresh fruit, and Alec suddenly realized how hungry he was.

The captain motioned Alec to a chair and sat down

himself, his back as straight as it had been in the saddle. For several minutes they ate in silence, then Alec asked, "Are you a student of Florida history as well as a professional horseman?" He nodded toward the books.

"Only recently," the captain answered. "I have learned from Odin that my people lived side by side with white men during the Spanish conquest of Florida. Of course it was as slaves," he added. There was no bitterness or hostility in his voice, only acceptance.

Alec waited expectantly, hoping the captain would tell him more of his own accord. He did not think it best to press him.

"In fact, one of my great ancestors was chief guide to the Conquistador Pedro Menéndez De Avillés," the captain continued after a short pause.

Alec detected the pride in the captain's voice.

"De Avillés was the founder of St. Augustine," the captain explained. "Unknown to most historians he also did a considerable amount of exploration here in the Everglades, which could not have been done without the aid of my ancestor who was a Carib warrior."

Alec was unable to keep the surprise from showing in his eyes. *Was this why the captain was here then, to retrace the steps of an ancestor dead over four hundred years?* He studied the man's face, noting again the strong blending of Negroid and Indian features, a blood mixture that became more complex with the addition of generations of still other nationalities.

The captain gazed back, his eyes as intent as Alec's. "You look surprised, Alec," he said quietly. "I might even say *frightened*. There is no need to think of one with Indian or, for that matter, Negro blood as a villain."

He paused before going on. "It is true that the Caribs were no less warlike than the Conquistadores. For they too were raiders, coming from the interior of the Guianas and as far south as the Amazon jungle. They invaded Haiti and the other islands before becoming slaves themselves. No different," he added, "than the African Negroes brought to the New World by the Spaniards to work the mines."

The captain stood up and began clearing the table. The conversation seemed to have come to an end. Suddenly he stopped and sat down again.

"So it is that I am of Carib blood as well as African and Portuguese and French and Haitian. Truly a strange mixture, *n'est-ce pas?*" he asked, smiling broadly for the first time.

"*Oui,* Captain," Alec answered, hoping that the tension between them had come to an end.

"*Comprenez-vous* French, Alec?"

"*Un peu.*"

"*Beaucoup* more than *un peu,* I'll bet," the captain said warmly.

Alec helped take the dishes into the kitchen. His feeling of apprehension had been greatly relieved by the friendly exchange.

"Your English is perfect," he said.

"Thank you. Not perfect but passable, I suppose. I have made many trips to England. Circus life makes it easy for one to learn languages." The captain began rinsing the dishes beneath the hand pump.

"And Odin?" Alec asked, wanting to learn more. "He lives here? You came here to see him?"

The captain's eyes became wary again but he did his best, Alec saw, to be pleasant. "Not quite," he answered. "Odin lives in Haiti. He knew of this hammock and we came here together."

There was no further explanation and Alec did not prod him. He was willing to wait. The captain was no longer the frightening man he had seemed; neither was Odin, whom Alec believed to be demented but harmless.

They finished the dishes and returned to the living room, where the captain motioned Alec to a chair beside him.

"It is good to have a professional horseman for company," he said. "I have always had great respect for one who rides a racing horse . . . not so much because of the speed itself, but to ride in the midst of others also fully extended calls for great skill and courage."

"A jockey has to take the dangers for granted and do the job," Alec answered. "I enjoy it. I wouldn't want to do anything else."

"Yes, you would have to enjoy it to live in the shadow of maiming and death with each race. What do you weigh?"

"About a hundred and fifteen."

"I am almost twice that and I would not enjoy it."

"You have other talents," Alec said, smiling. With the talk of horses all tension had left him.

"Yes, I prefer to *make* a horse rather than *break* one.

The mouths of all your horses are as hard as the iron you put in them."

"Not necessarily," Alec said, surprised at his quick anger. "The Black's mouth has not been made hard. He responds to the slightest touch and I use my hands and legs the same as you . . . not as well, perhaps, or the same way," he added more cautiously. "Yet I think we get the same results."

The captain smiled at his outburst and, it seemed to Alec, that the difference in their ages was fast disappearing.

"If what you say is true, Alec, your horse not only serves you as a race horse but shares his life with you."

They were interrupted as Odin crossed the room, opened the door without a glance in their direction, and went out. Alec noted that he was no longer wearing the crimson robe with the gold braid, but the black felt hat still covered his head. However, without the robe and the spear-tipped rod, he did not look so ominous.

The captain's gaze left the closed door and returned to Alec. "You are alone with your horse in Florida?" he asked.

"Alone?" Alec repeated. "No, not exactly." He offered no further explanation, thinking that if the captain was inquisitive enough about him and his horse, he might be able to trade information. He wanted to know why a famous horseman like the captain was living on a remote hammock in the Everglades.

"You said Odin goes where he pleases. Aren't you worried?" he asked.

"No. I also told you he is very capable. He knows the swamp better than I do, and he is familiar with the Seminole tongue so he has made friends in the nearby Indian village." The captain paused, as-if undecided whether to continue. A light flickered in his dark eyes, then, having made his decision, he went on. "Like the Seminoles, Odin is suspicious of the outside world. Lately, his antagonism seems to be directed toward the white men who are draining the Everglades. It is for that reason I told him you were my friend and asked you to take his hand."

"I can understand his feelings," Alec said. "But I don't believe the engineers will ever conquer the swamp. It's too immense."

"Perhaps you are right," the captain said quietly, "but they're making progress. I too resent and challenge this conquest by the white man. It will not be long before . . ."

The captain stopped abruptly as if, perhaps, he had said too much. There was a haunted look in his eyes and Alec wondered what had caused it.

"But enough of such talk, Alec. We must continue with out discussion of you and your horse. You said you were not alone?"

Alec smiled to himself. The trade of information had begun and now it was his turn.

"I'm not alone in that we're staying at Sugarfoot Ranch," he said. "We've been there a little over a week, resting up after racing at Hialeah Park in Miami. My partner and trainer, Henry Dailey, went up north a few days ago to look after some two-year-olds, but he'll be back within a week. Then we go to New York to prepare for the spring racing season at Aqueduct."

"I see," the captain said, his eyes once more becoming hard and cold. "Then you *are* alone with your horse."

Alec felt his uneasiness return. He didn't know what the captain meant. They'd be expecting him back at the ranch by afternoon, and he certainly wasn't alone. Whatever thoughts the captain had were locked up tightly inside him. Yet Alec found that he no longer distrusted him as he had earlier. Slowly he was acquiring more and more information and the pieces were fitting together. Soon he'd come up with the whole picture.

"Racing is a rough business," he told the captain. "We're on the go most of the time. I suppose it's much like circus work."

"I suppose so. Neither is the work for timid souls."

"Timid?" Alec repeated. "I hadn't thought of it that way. But you're right. If you're going to race like a lady, you might as well stay home."

"Timidity has no place in the circus either," the captain said quietly. "Let me show you some old prints I have here."

He went to a trunk near the fireplace and removed a thick folder. From it he took some pictures and spread them on the table. Alec saw horses and riders leaping through hoops of fire and over the backs of elephants and tigers. The prints dated back to the early 1800s. There was one that intrigued him more than the others. It showed a beautiful white horse wearing simulated wings and flying over four horses standing below.

"This is supposed to be Pegasus?" he asked the captain.

"*Oui,* Alec. It was performed by Antonio Franconi in 1800 in London. The mythical winged horse was very popular with audiences of the time."

Alec noted that the large wings were attached to a light girth strap. Truly, the horse appeared to be flying, and he could understand why it had been a successful act. The pity of it was that such a mythical figure would not be accepted in today's circus because people did not accept fantasy as part of their world. The simulated wings on a leaping horse would only evoke laughter, not excitement.

When Alec mentioned this to the captain, the man asked, "But *you,* Alec, do you believe there is some basis of fact to mythology?"

"Perhaps more than most people do," Alec said honestly. "At least I've thought about it a lot, especially Pegasus. I used to ride a make-believe winged horse as a kid. He took me all over the world."

"I suspected as much," the captain said. "And now that you're no longer a child, what do you think of such mythical creatures? Were they only imaginary? Was there no basis of fact for them?"

Alec thought a minute and then said, "I've read that primitive men credited many animals with powers far beyond their own. I think it was even believed that their gods took on animal form when they descended to earth." He smiled. "I suppose that's how Pegasus came about. Is that what you mean?"

"*Oui,* in part, Alec," the captain said, his gaze returning to the print before him. "But you must remember that until quite recently mankind continued to believe in a magical world in which animal and human shapes were *interchangeable.*" He picked up the print, studying it. "Not all the animals were as beautiful as Pegasus. Some were so horrible that men would die in terror at the very sight of them."

The captain's voice was solemn but Alec could not take him seriously. It was part of an act, put on for his benefit, he decided. He laughed and said, "They were fairy tales, Captain, told since the beginning of time. People don't believe in them any more, not in this day and age."

"That's part of the trouble," the captain said.

Alec believed him to mean that for this reason there was no place for a horse with simulated wings in the circus ring.

The captain added, "However, it is possible that some legendary creatures were based on animals which did actually *exist.*"

"I can believe that," Alec said. "The fierce dragon was the result of prehistoric man finding fossils of dinosaurs or any of the other reptilian monsters."

"But what of the *supernatural* animals?" the captain asked quietly. "What of the *gryphon,* half eagle and half lion? And the *hippogriff* who had the body of a horse and the wings and beak of an eagle, and the claws of a lion? Medieval writers had no doubt that such animals existed."

"Purely imaginary," Alec answered, "no different than the centaur, half man and half horse . . . and all the other creatures of fable, created by the ancients."

"Perhaps so," the captain said, picking up another old print and passing it on to Alec.

It showed a man in a circus ring, dressed as the devil and driving what must have been at least twenty horses while standing on the backs of the two in the rear.

"Another imaginary figure," Alec said, pointing to the devil-clad man. "But it's quite a feat, driving that many horses. I wonder if he actually did it."

"He did," the captain said. "My great-grandfather saw him perform in the Paris Hippodrome in 1860."

There were hundreds of prints in the bulging folder, all of performing horses and some going as far back as the Circus Maximus at the time of Christ. To anyone it would have been a fascinating and valuable collection; for Alec, a serious horseman, it was the like of which he had never hoped to see. And, with the captain explaining the techniques of the training involved, the hours passed without his being aware of it.

The long rumble of thunder interrupted his concentration on the old prints and made him conscious of the time. He glanced at his watch and rose quickly to his feet. "I had no idea it was so late," he said. "It's after four and I must be going. Thanks for lunch and everything." He glanced at the prints. "Maybe I can come back?" He put it as a question, sensing that the captain preferred solitude to the company of another person. In a way they were very much alike, disdaining the company of other men for that of their horses.

Yet, Alec thought, how strange it was that he wanted to return when he had been so alarmed before. He looked into the captain's dark, unblinking eyes as the man rose to join him.

"You are welcome any time," the captain said, "but I had hoped you would stay even longer."

The rays of the sun were still streaming through the small windows but there was another clap of thunder in the distance.

"I don't want to get caught in a storm," Alec said. "I'll get back late as it is. They'll be worrying about me."

Alec opened the door and the heat outside was scorching. To the south, just above the saw-grass spears, a heavy blanket of clouds shone in a bizarre light.

"I doubt it will rain, as much as we need it," the captain said, following Alec down the steps. "Perhaps some wind and heat lightning but no rain certainly. I feel none in the air."

Alec shrugged his shoulders. "The lightning will be quite bad enough," he said. "I don't mind getting wet— it's lightning that really shakes me up."

"You're afraid?" the captain asked, a note of surprise in his voice. "You who have the courage to race?"

Alec smiled at the comparison but did not slow his strides. "A storm and a race are two different things," he said, "calling for two different kinds of courage, if you wish to call it that. I'm afraid of lightning because I've seen too many animals killed in pasture by it, and my horse and I have had some terrible experiences in storms. They're not easy to forget."

"Then I wish you would stay," the captain said hopefully. "You may be right about this storm. See how the thunderheads are coming this way!"

Alec glanced at the sky to the south, then back to meet the captain's searching gaze. He wasn't afraid of him any longer but something brooded in those eyes. They held a hooded look, as if the man wanted something, but would not divulge what it was.

Was it that he and the captain were wary and suspicious of each other, friendly but on guard? There was no doubt that the captain wanted him to stay, and perhaps that had been his intention when he'd shown him the old prints. But why did the captain want him there when it was evident that he was most happy alone? Otherwise, he would not be in such a remote place.

There was much Alec wanted to know but he had run out of time. Perhaps, as he'd told the captain, he'd come back another day. His strides lengthened until he was in a half-run. He wanted to reach his horse and get away immediately. It would give him time to decide whether or not he should return at all.

6 · The Storm

Thunder rolled and the fast-moving clouds began to blot out the afternoon sun. Alec ran faster toward the shed where he had left the Black. A storm had brought him and his horse together and he'd never forget it. There had been other storms during his travels, almost as bad, and he knew how he reacted to them. It was not a softness he was ashamed of but an acceptance of a new way of life. His fear of storms was locked tightly inside him and he could do nothing about it.

"At least wait until the storm passes," the captain said, running alongside.

"I think I'll be able to make it."

"As you wish," the captain answered.

A ragged, violet lightning flash split the sky as they approached the shed. It shook them both and Alec could not hide the fear in his eyes.

"You'll never be able to outride it," the captain said. "You and your horse will be much safer under cover. It might well be over in a few minutes."

Alec looked southward. The wind was increasing and lightning flashes were crackling over the saw-grass sea. If he started out and lost his sense of direction he'd really be in trouble. Yet if he stayed he doubted he'd be able to get away until very late. It did not look like the kind of storm that would be over in a few minutes.

His decision to remain was made just as another flash of lightning came from the cloud cover almost directly overhead. It was dead white, and Alec had no time to involuntarily duck his head or even collect his wits as a thunderbolt crashed, seemingly a few feet to his right. It roared in his ears as he and the captain made a mad dash for the shed doors.

A second blaze of lightning brightened the area when the captain pulled open the doors. "*Vite*, Alec, quickly, inside!" he shouted. They stepped inside and closed the doors behind them.

The Black nickered and Alec went to him quickly. Storms affected the Black just as they affected him; each offered the other solace at such times. Whenever possible, Alec was with him during a bad storm. His hand rubbed the muscled ridge of the Black's neck.

There was another crash of thunder, and the light coming through the open window was eerie. Frequent flashes brightened the sky and Alec could see huge thunderheads marching up from the south.

"Rain should come soon now," he said. "It might not be so bad then."

The captain did not take his eyes from the window. "I smell no rain, only the electricity in the air," he answered.

A spurt of violet fire brightened the shed and they saw a tall cabbage palm split in two and fall to the ground. There was another flash and still another. The earth and sky were being joined in flaming white charges while thunder crashed incessantly.

Alec's fingers tightened on the Black's mane. He could not tell his horse there was nothing to fear, that it was not like the first time. Actually it was worse, except that they were not in a ship at sea.

One did not forget a ship rolling helplessly in monstrous seas and raging winds while jarring cracks of lightning split her open. A dead ship, her engines long quiet, going deeper into the water.

"I have never known the fear of a storm," the captain said quietly, as if intent on distracting Alec's thoughts. "We circus people are used to all kinds of dangers, traveling and living in so many strange countries as we do. One must go where one can earn a living."

Alec turned to him. He knew the captain's words were meant to be warm and friendly, to get his mind off the storm. His fear must be quite apparent, then.

"Your mare must be a good traveler," he said, willing to talk about anything that would pass the time.

"*Oui,* she has had to be," the captain answered, "as it

is with all circus animals. However, she is better than most, I believe. She is a seasoned traveler, very worldly indeed."

The Black moved uneasily as a loud rumble of thunder shook the shed. Alec steadied him with his hands. The thunderheads seemed to be closer, pressing down upon the hammock. Still there was no rain—only the wind and lightning and thunder.

"Perhaps you don't fear it because you have never known what a tropical storm is like," Alec commented.

"Perhaps so, Alec," the captain answered. "It is not often that we travel so far south. Usually we are in Europe at this time of year. But in so much of the Continent today there is no time for the circus. In Germany, for example, the circus is almost dead. Perhaps it is due to television—or, perhaps, to there not being enough children. The circus is for children, you know. In Ireland last year it was very good. There is not much television in Ireland and there are many children."

Amid the crashes of thunder, the lightning made the world of saw grass outside leap vividly into sight, with one green ball of fire after another brightening the darkness. It was weird and frightening. One lightning bolt missed the shed by what seemed like a few yards, and for a dizzy moment Alec felt the tingle of static electricity in his body.

He heard the captain's voice and was astounded to find him still talking about his work.

"Do you think Americans will be pleased with my act?" the captain asked.

Alec was quick to note the slight hesitancy in his

voice that betrayed his worldliness and contempt for the storm.

"I think they'll like your mare very much," he said. "Americans love horses and will appreciate one so well trained as yours."

He had no sooner spoken than a great flash of lightning bathed the inside of the shed in an eerie garish light. He held his breath, expecting the earth to erupt beneath his feet; his hands tightened around the Black's neck.

The roof of the shed toppled but was held from falling by two wooden beams.

Alec looked up at the sagging roof. "It'll hold," he said. "A tree must have fallen on it."

When the captain spoke, his voice was charged with emotion he could not control. "It would take a man of iron not to fear such force as this," he said shakily. "We are indeed in the hands of the gods."

Alec turned to the window and watched the giant black thunderheads move overhead. He expected them to bring heavy rain and provide a respite from the fearful bolts of lightning. They marched by in what seemed to be never-ending columns and brought only a slight drizzle instead of the deluge he had expected. The lightning never lessened in its intensity. The saw-grass world was lit up with successive flashes and Alec knew that if it did not rain, the Everglades might well be destroyed by fire from the bolts.

He ducked instinctively as another ball of green fire shattered the darkness. The captain said not a word. There was a deep silence between him and Alec. Their lives had whittled down to a grim, waiting battle for survival. They could only wait and pray and hope the lightning would not strike the shed.

The storm went on for a long time, longer than Alec ever had known one to last. There seemed to be no end to the fury of the wind and fierce lightning. It was almost as if the wrath of the heavens had been turned against them instead of the storm's being a natural phenomenon of clouds and barometric pressures.

It was night when, finally, the storm came to an end. Alec watched the sky clear and saw the first stars; he gave no thought to where he was . . . or to the captain . . . or going home or staying. Nothing mattered except that he and his horse had survived. He led the Black from the shed and walked about the clearing, avoiding the fallen trees.

The captain passed him, his eyes unfocused and staring. Alec knew where he was going and followed. They found the barn and house intact. It seemed incredible, when everything else was a shambles. No doubt the tall trees, serving as lightning deflectors, had saved them.

While the captain went inside the barn to his mare, Alec waited and spoke to the Black without benefit of a spoken word, his touches soft and gentle.

Finally the captain emerged from the barn, striding quickly toward them. Alec had only to look at the captain's face to know that the mare was safe. Despite the difference in their ages and backgrounds, he and the captain had a deep bond in common for each was one with his horse.

"It's too late for you to leave now," the captain said. "You'll have to spend the night."

Alec nodded. He could not attempt the long trip in the darkness. "They'll wonder what happened to me," he said. "They'll be worried."

"We can avoid that," the captain said quickly. "I'll have Odin take a message, at least as far as the Seminole village; his friends will see that it's delivered to the ranch."

"You're sure?" Alec asked, surprised that anyone could find his way through the swamp at night.

"Of course," the captain said. "There will be no problem. He has a canoe and goes by the waterways."

The night was still except for the fronds of palm trees rattling ominously in the wind. The air was cool, for the storm had driven off the intense heat. To the north, Alec could see skittering sheets of lightning, flashing luridly, then vanishing in the night sky.

"Where will we put him?" he asked, nodding toward his horse. "The shed's not safe. The roof could fall in any time."

"There are several stalls in the barn," the captain answered. "We will put him there."

Alec didn't like it. The mare was so ready to be bred. His concern must have been obvious, for the captain said, "You needn't worry. I can put him at the far end of the barn, well away from her."

"All right," Alec said resignedly.

Later, he walked beside the captain through the evening shadows. He had spent the last hour as he would have done at home, putting up his horse for the night. He had brushed him off and cleaned his feet. He had fetched water and hay for him and put his bed straight. He had made sure the stall door was locked, so there was no possibility of the Black's getting to the mare—but he knew his horse's squeals would go on most of the night. There was nothing more to be done except wait for morning when he could leave.

He wondered if it had been a mistake to stay. Perhaps he should have tried to make it, even going with Odin part of the way. But he didn't trust the old man. A short while ago, he had seen him disappear into the gravelike hush of the swamp, taking to the Seminole village the message which the captain had given him. No, Alec decided, he would not have wanted to go along with Odin.

Yet how much safer was he here? Alec tried to shrug off this line of thought. It was silly to think he was in any danger. He was with another horseman who was good enough to put him up for the night.

A mist hung over the silver-blue sheen of the swamp; the stars shone like primrose diamonds in the heavens. It was really a very beautiful night. Nothing moved. Nothing stirred. One should feel a great peace on such a night, and yet . . .

Alec felt no peace, only a sudden dread. He tried to shake it off and couldn't. He had the crazy thought that the captain would *not* have let him leave the hammock even if it hadn't been for the storm. Why did the captain want him there?

The strange house where he must spend the night loomed before him.

7 · *Images and Omens*

Alec was given a bedroom on the second floor. After washing, he went to the open window that looked out over the swamp to the south and west. He still had no idea why the captain was in the Everglades. It had to be for reasons other than privacy, although, Alec admitted to himself, it was for that too. Was it, as well, to retrace the steps of his long-dead ancestor, the guide to a Spanish Conquistador? If so, *why?*

Alec could feel the throbbing in his temples; he knew it to be a self-warning of danger despite the aura of peace and quiet that had settled over the hammock and the swamp.

71

Why did he feel the need to be so alert when every-thing appeared to be perfectly all right? The message had been sent to Sugarfoot Ranch. In the light of early morning, he would be on his way back.

Yet appearances were deceptive, and the captain was anything but normal. Alec remained at the window, his face silhouetted against the light, breathing in the night air.

He wasn't afraid, he told himself, only concerned and cautious. If he had been afraid, he would have been able to smell his fear; it had a scent of its own and was unmistakable. He hated it.

He had every right to be suspicious. He couldn't be certain Odin had taken the message to the Indian village and that it would reach the ranch. However, there was nothing he could do about it except to be alert every minute he remained on the hammock. Caution was not cowardice. Caution was born of wisdom that he had acquired the hard way. Like the captain, he too was a professional.

Alec gazed at the vast expanse of saw grass and won-dered how much of it was tinder-dry. The afternoon storm had done little to relieve the drought but at least it was the forerunner of the wet season to come when torrential rains would help keep the Everglades alive.

He saw no evidence of smoke or fire as a result of the lightning. Yet he knew that in some areas the deep de-posits of peat soil were powder-dry and, once ignited, might smolder for days, if not weeks. There was always the danger of the sea of grass becoming a sea of fire from such a storm. It was not a prospect to make one feel at ease. He turned away from the window and left the room.

He had reached the top of the dimly lit stairs when he heard the music. It was very faint at first, then it swelled, mounting to a clash of cymbals before fading away again.

Alec started down the stairs. The captain must be playing a record on the phonograph he had seen earlier. The music had a strange, dreamlike quality.

He heard a thin, haunting piping sound and, despite his knowing that he was listening to a record, a shiver went up his back. It was a long flute passage, mysterious and remote, and yet he was certain he had heard it before!

Alec came to a dead stop, for the music suddenly created a feeling that *something* was about to happen. The haunting flute passage ended but other sounds from other instruments came to him in the darkness of the stairs, taking him far beyond the house to the outer world of stars and distant solitude.

He shook his head, trying to rid himself of the strange mood that had come over him. It was weird music, almost uncanny. The notes seemed to have receding echoes, giving him the distinct impression that he was listening to the shrill cries of distant birds. It was ominous music and yet he found he was not frightened by it. Instead it brought to him a feeling of excitement, an intoxicating sense of danger, of challenge!

The flute passage began again. He listened to the shrill, piping notes, wondering why they sounded familiar to him. He could not have explained the way he felt except by saying that he seemed to be suspended in some kind of dream.

There had to be a reason for the familiarity of the notes. He sought it desperately, knowing that the explanation would shake the unreal mood that held him. The answer finally came to him.

The bird notes he had heard on his way here! The notes had followed him for a short while. Actually he had never seen the bird, if it had been a bird at all.

The music quickened and Alec's heart raced with it. Perhaps it was only a coincidence that the haunting notes of the flute were similar to the ones he had heard in the brush; yet the similarity alarmed him. He smelled his own fear.

The music came to an end but it was a full minute before Alec moved. Only when he heard the unmistakable sounds of the captain removing the record from the turntable did he continue down the stairs. When he entered the large living room he had regained control of himself.

The captain, searching Alec's eyes to learn his reaction to the weird music, shifted his gaze to Alec's hands. Alec quickly unclenched them. He had no intention of letting the man know what he was thinking; his thoughts were part of himself and very private. He moved easily across the room to the phonograph and glanced at the record.

"I've never heard more *ghostly* music," he said.

"Many find it frightening," the captain answered, his

voice oddly deep. He placed the record on a high shelf.

"I'm not surprised," Alec said quietly.

For the first time, he noticed the twitching of a muscle on the right side of the captain's cheek. Evidently the man wasn't as relaxed as he pretended to be. It made it easier for Alec to meet the captain's eyes.

"Although I helped write the music," the captain continued, "there are times when it frightens me, too." He smiled slightly and put a hand on Alec's arm, leading him across the room to the high-backed chairs beside the fireplace.

"You're a composer as well?" Alec asked, impressed. Frightening as the music had been, he recognized its high quality.

"Oh, no, Alec," the captain said. He lit the oil lamp overhead. "It's the only music I've ever written and it happened quite by accident. Well, if not by accident, under rather strange circumstances. Would you like to hear about it?"

Alec sensed the captain's mood and knew he would go on without any encouragement from him, but he nodded anyway.

Several seconds passed before the captain spoke again. "I have no musical talent but like most circus performers I have always given intense thought to the music that accompanies my act." His dark eyes were staring into space. "In many ways the music is as important as the training, for it creates the mood to which performers, as well as the audience, respond.

"Years ago, I had a friend in Paris, a remarkable music

teacher, a man of great skill and talent. I told André of my new act and asked him for music that would give my mare the necessary cues for her movements and, at the same time, create an ethereal, ghostlike mood . . ."

The captain paused, his eyes becoming focused on Alec again. "You see, Alec, she works alone in the ring."

"*Alone*," Alec repeated, ". . . without your hands and legs to guide her? I wouldn't think it possible."

"Her cues are set to music, as I have said," the captain went on quickly and with pride. "Not easy, of course, but I have accomplished it. She works in a dim spotlight in a darkened arena. It is most effective."

"I should think so," Alec said, impressed.

"She is called *The Ghost*. Do you think it is a little too frightening for Americans?"

"Not at all," Alec said, smiling and feeling more at ease. "Ghosts are popular in America, too."

"*Bon*, that is fine, for I did not want to change it. But to return to my music. I told André that I must have an original composition, something entirely different to create the mood I wanted for *La Fantôme*.

"I recall pacing his studio, trying to explain to him what I meant. I began humming to help transfer my thoughts to music. And, as always when I'm perplexed, I began rubbing the little figurine which I have carried since I was a small boy."

The captain paused, a large hand digging into his pants pocket. He held a small image before Alec's eyes. "This is she," he said in a confiding tone, ". . . without her I would be nothing."

Alec stared in astonishment at the grotesque object in

the captain's hand. It was yellow and might well have been solid gold. Even so, it was not the value of the figurine that startled him but the large head with the small green eyes and the long pointed ears. The body was frightening too, for it was thin and horribly twisted, as if she—if it could be called a female figure—was in agony.

Never in Alec's life had he seen a more ugly, evil-looking object. He tried to keep the disgust from his face for the captain was holding the figurine lovingly in his large black hands. Only when his fingers closed over the figurine, shutting it off from Alec's view, did he resume his story.

"You must understand, Alec," he went on, his tone still confiding, "that André was a man to whom music was the most important thing in life. He had no use for would-be musicians like myself. Nevertheless, he listened to my humming a long while and then he said, *'Philip, you are a most peculiar man in many ways.'*

"Then he asked me to continue my humming while he put the notes down on paper. At first, I thought he meant it just as a gesture. But he was serious, and in a moment I had lost my self-consciousness and the melody came effortlessly, almost of its own accord. I recall feeling very strange at the time and yet being very calm about it.

"The only thing that mattered," the captain went on, "was that I knew the tune was exactly right for the mood I'd hoped to create. André knew it, too. He asked me to repeat it time and time again. I had no trouble obliging him for it was as if I had always known it."

The captain's gaze met Alec's. "This I know now to be true, Alec. The melody itself was deep in my subconscious, some memory of my parents' or grandparents' singing when I was a child, its origin more Carib Indian than Haitian or African. All my life I have obeyed the promptings of my inner self and it has accounted for much of what I have accomplished in my work. No one else would have dared attempt to train a high school horse to obey musical cues!"

Alec wanted to look away from the captain's unblinking gaze but couldn't, so he nodded his head in full agreement. He must not make an enemy of this man. Nothing was as simple as it sounded but he'd better believe the captain if he wanted to remain friends with him.

"André completed the arrangements, writing parts for all the instruments, and we had an original composition of breath-taking beauty so right for my act."

Alec said nothing, not thinking it wise to bring up the *fearful* quality of the music as well. He watched the curled fingers of the man's hand open and once again the gold figurine was exposed to his view.

"Do you believe in the powers of the *supernatural,* Alec?" the captain asked softly.

Alec tried to shrug off a sudden feeling of dread. He said half-jokingly, "I carry a good-luck piece like a lot of other superstitious jockeys, if that's what you mean."

"I mean much more than that," the captain said. "Do you believe in sins and omens?"

"I suppose everyone feels he's had a premonition now and then of something that might happen. But to answer your question, no, I don't believe in signs and omens, Captain."

"It is not your nature to believe as it is mine," the captain said. "I am more superstitious than most men. I believe strongly in her powers." He raised the figurine to Alec's face. "I must never let her fall into unkind hands."

Again Alec fought the impulse to turn away from the frightening ugliness of the image. He must not let the captain know how he felt. He stared into the figurine's green eyes held opposite his own. They seemed to be winking back at him. He knew his imagination was playing tricks on him but he didn't turn away. Why did the captain want to know how much he could take before he revealed his fears openly?

The green eyes continued winking and Alec had no idea how many minutes he looked into them before the captain put the figurine back in his pocket.

"It has been in my family for many, many generations," the captain said, his voice now more matter-of-fact. "Strangely enough, some of my ancestors believed— as does Odin—that it was found in an Indian burial mound not far from this hammock."

Alec closed his eyes for a few seconds and lightly pressed his fingers over his lids. One more piece had been fitted into the puzzle, he thought. The captain had returned to the area where his beloved figurine was believed to have been found. But Alec no longer cared to learn the reason *why*. All he wished was that he had never ridden to the hammock.

He didn't want the captain to confide in him, whatever reason the man might have for doing it. Alec had a premonition of his own now. He knew too much already and, if he learned more, he might never be allowed to leave.

"I like you, Alec," the captain was saying softly. "You are a very imaginative person. You would not have come this way today if you were not. While you are practical about many things, you often live in a magical world. Am I not right?"

"No more than others I know," Alec said. "Having an imagination is part of living. I came this way because I had never seen the real Everglades and I was curious."

"Of course," the captain answered. The ghost of a smile reappeared on his thick lips. "You are young so you are imaginative and curious. Most adults lose both very quickly in their attempts to be useful and practical. There are few who believe there is anything that might ever excel, even surpass, life itself!"

Alec studied the captain's intent face, wondering how far he could go. Finally he said, "You must be kidding. Even young people wouldn't go so far as to believe that."

There was no humor in the masklike face before him, and Alec knew he had miscalculated when the captain's dark eyes burned into his own. He should have kept quiet. He believed now that he was coping with a man not completely sane.

Their gazes held and Alec did his best not to betray his convictions. Finally the captain smiled and the tension was broken. "You have nothing to fear from me, Alec. I make no apologies for my beliefs and I certainly do not want you to forgive me for them. Please do not look at me as if I were a mentally sick person and you must humor me. That is too much, and I would like us to continue being friends."

Alec was startled by the ease with which the captain had read his mind and even more by the direct accusation. "I meant no criticism of you or what you believe in," he said quickly. "One lives according to his own beliefs, not those of others."

"*Très bien,* that is what I hoped you'd say! You are a very tolerant fellow, Alec."

Alec wondered where such a conversation was leading and how he'd ever get through the night. He tried to read the captain's face.

"It is for that reason I wanted you to stay," the captain said.

Alec smiled, surprised at his courage in confrontation with this man. "Because you believe I am a very tolerant fellow?" he asked. "Only that?"

"Of course, Alec," the captain said kindly, staring at him fixedly. "You are the kind of person who would not think it a complete waste of time to pursue another's fantasies even though you did not believe in them yourself."

"And that is important to you?" Alec asked.

"*Oui,* it is important to me," the captain repeated. "I have waited a long time to tell someone what I know to be true. But what more I have to say can wait until we have had our dinner. I have talked long enough for now."

Alec watched the captain rise from his chair, his tall

body moving easily and with perfect coordination. He strode toward the kitchen like a tiger in motion.

What more did the captain mean to tell him? Alec wondered. His muscles felt tense and he sought to relax them by getting to his feet and walking around the room. He must be ready to move in any direction at a second's notice. He had no intention of being easy prey to a man who had the stealth and cunning of a jungle animal. He would have to be on guard every moment during the long night to come.

8 · The Legend

"I believe in a world that is far from ordinary," the captain told Alec after dinner, "one that transcends anything yet conceived or even considered by serious and practical people. If I told them what I tell you, they would think me mad."

Alec said nothing. All through dinner he had done little but listen to the captain speak of images and symbols that had guided the course of his life. His was more a dark world of mystery and fantasy than one of imagination, pure and simple. The captain might well be a citizen of France but his Haitian ancestry was the root and essence of all he believed.

"I have not lived in vain, Alec," the captain went on, "for I have proof of everything I have told you."

"But why tell me?" Alec asked. "I do not believe all this."

"Because your coming here is one of the signs," the captain replied quietly.

"In what way?"

"When I saw your horse on Swedish television, I knew I would find him in America. Truthfully, I did not expect our paths to cross in this swamp but now I realize it could not have been otherwise."

"But why my horse?" Alec asked. He knew the answer and was only biding for time. It had been evident from the moment the captain had set eyes upon the Black that he coveted him for his mare.

"Your horse is worthy of *La Fantôme,* and I would like her to have a foal," the captain said.

"The Black can't be used now," Alec said, surprised at the cold defiance in his voice. He saw quick anger come to the man's eyes and added more warily, "You must understand, Captain. You're a horseman. I don't have to tell you what using him now would mean."

Alec searched the captain's face for understanding but found none; there was only a creeping coldness that was more frightening than anger would have been. He knew now why the captain had wanted him to stay. It had nothing to do with companionship; this man had no need for the company of others. It was only his horse the captain wanted.

The man stared steadily at Alec for a long while. Then he spoke and, surprisingly, his voice was kind. "Of

course I understand, Alec. As you say, I am a professional horseman like yourself. We must have patience
to get what we want, *n'est-ce pas?* Later, then?"

"Yes, later," Alec repeated. "There'll be no problem
when the racing season is over." For a moment he felt
that he could cope with this man if they continued to
talk of horses. He sought to keep to the subject.

"You will be without an act when she's with foal,"
he said.

The captain shrugged. *"Oui,"* he agreed. "But she has
worked a long time. She is not young any more. I will
use another horse or, perhaps, I will wait until her colt
is old enough to train."

"It might be a filly," Alec suggested. "Then you'd
have a mare to take her place."

"I hope not. A stallion is easier, much easier than a
mare to train for the ring."

Alec shook his head. "I don't follow you," he said.
"I can't see a stallion being as tractable as your mare, especially one with the Black in him. He'd blow up in
the ring."

"No, Alec," the captain said. "With a stallion there
is just one fight, always at the beginning. When he
learns that you are his master, it is over and the rest is
easy. With most mares the fight is never over."

Alec said, "I suppose it depends on the temperament
of the stallion."

"Of course, some fight longer than others but in the
end they all become obedient. They quickly learn to
avoid punishment while mares do not."

"You can't punish the Black," Alec said. "You can ask

and even be firm, but if you fight him, he'll fight back."

"That's part of training, Alec," the captain said, his eyes suddenly afire. "But *you* must win. There is no other way. A horse is the slave to man, not his master."

Alec dropped his gaze, reminding himself once more that he must not antagonize this man. At times the captain seemed sensible, even friendly, but he was always dangerous. Alec warned himself not to forget it for a moment.

Suddenly the captain sprang to his feet, lightly, silently, and again Alec was reminded of a jungle cat as he watched him go over to the trunk beside the fireplace.

"Now I will show you more, Alec," he called from across the room, "much more." He removed the thick folder and returned to the table.

Sitting down again, he pulled out all the papers in the folder and spread them across the table for Alec to see. In addition to the circus prints Alec had seen that afternoon, there were handwritten notes and some legal-looking documents with signs and figures and coat of arms. Most of them were in old-fashioned handwriting, in Spanish and French and still other languages that Alec did not recognize. There were musty drawings of strange, weird creatures, half-man, half-animal; primitive art of the kind a child might draw. All were very old for the ink was faded and the papers tissue-thin.

The captain's face bore the look of one on a great adventure and his eyes burned with intensity.

"These records tell of the old race from which I come," he said. "A few were in my possession before I visited

Haiti. It was there I found Odin and he had the others hidden away, given to him by his father and to his father before him, to the beginning of . . ."

He checked himself and paused a moment, as if undecided how much to tell Alec. Finally he continued. "The first of these old records was made by my ancestor who was chief guide to the Conquistador Pedro Menendez De Avillés.

"It is an account of what happened in Florida and the record was passed on to his son who, it was said, had powers out of the ordinary in Haiti. He was regarded as being very strong and fearless by his people, even worshiped by some. He was half Carib Indian and half African, a most potent mixture of bloods."

The captain paused again and his dark eyes had a far-off look, as if some strong feeling stirred within him. Alec detected too a quick flash of fear as if he thought he might be betraying a secret and would have to pay the consequences. Nevertheless, after a moment the captain continued.

"It was he who made his way to this swamp and lived here for many years before returning to Haiti. Most of these drawings were done by him."

The captain picked one up, studying it carefully. "He brought back a legend that has been passed on from generation to generation in my family. Even I considered it full of impossible events but it remained with me always."

Alec was moved by the emotion he saw in the man's face, and despite his self-warning to be cautious, he knew that the captain's excitement was being transmitted to himself. It was as if the captain had entered a magical world with new and unheard-of joys in the offing. Yet there could also be new and unheard-of *dangers!* Alec turned away. He wanted no part of the captain's strange, undiscovered world.

Finally, against his will, he turned back. The captain had gone to the darkened window. On his face was a look of haunted longing for someone or something he desperately wanted to see. Alec was stirred again by emotions he did not understand. He glanced out the window himself, half expecting to see a vision, anything that would account for the strange feeling he had that there was a persistent calling coming from outside. But there was nothing beyond the open window, only the blackness of the night. Not a whisper came from the swamp.

"The legend is of *Koví,* believed by my people to be one of the most powerful of all supernatural beings," the captain said quietly without turning to Alec. "It was said that he swept through the trees like a giant firefly, his belly flashing, with smoke and flame pouring from his mouth and nostrils."

"And you believe this?" Alec asked incredulously.

"I believe what I have been told," the captain answered. "As I have said, Alec, mine is an old race with old beliefs and mysteries; I would not expect you to believe them."

He turned away from the window, his eyes meeting Alec's. "Nor should you," he went on, "for they are not of the ordinary."

"Then why are you telling me?" Alec asked. The Haitian people were well known for their supernatural beliefs, some as strong today as they were in the time of the captain's ancestors.

"I am not sure why I tell you this," the captain answered. "It is, perhaps, simply that you are here as I am here. It might 'be for the reason that you too are a professional horseman. The signs may have shown you the way here as they did me."

Alec dropped his gaze. The captain gave the impression he had embarked on some great and marvelous adventure. Alec had no desire to go along. He tried to decide what best to do. Again he warned himself not to antagonize this man. He must hang on to the lingering belief that the captain, despite his supernatural beliefs, meant him no harm.

"Do you mean the legend has to do with horses?" Alec asked.

"Very much so," the captain answered. "My people looked upon horses as gods returning to earth in animal form. They ran in terror before the mounted Spaniards, believing them to have supernatural powers that enabled them to control the god-horses.

"However, my great ancestor, the chief guide to De Avillés, knew the horses were animals and, according to his records, wanted a mount of his own. De Avillés promised him a horse if he would betray his people by leading the Spaniards into the swamp where the Caribs were hiding. This he did quickly and with no remorse.

"During the attack, the Caribs in their terror and need called upon *Kovi* for help. They asked him to destroy those who had gained control over the god-horses. It is written in the records that *Kovi* answered by bring-

ing swift death to the invaders, and upon my great
ancestor fell the most dreadful fate of all. Upon him
and his family the curse of *Kovi,* a fear and suffering
worse than death itself, would forever remain."

"That's primitive nonsense," Alec said.

"Perhaps I would think as you do," the captain answered, "if Odin had not convinced me otherwise. When
I arrived in Haiti a month ago, he was dying. I found
him on the floor of his hut, his body twisted in agony
and his flesh as cold as death. I thought him dead until
I opened his eyelids and found him staring at me in
mortal terror. He seemed to know who I was, for his
twisted body, which I had thought paralyzed, uncoiled
with the lithe movement of a snake, and he jumped to
his feet.

"I hardly knew what he was up to when he grabbed
the figurine from my hand. As I have told you, I often
hold it when I'm under any kind of stress or strain. I
attempted to get it back from him, telling him who I
was, but he continued to look at me in horror, as if he
believed some terrible thing about me. It was then, too,
I realized that his twisted body was not unlike that of
the figurine.

"He began to speak in a kind of monotone, never
taking his eyes from mine. I barely understood him. It
sounded as if he were warning me of something from
which there was no escape. There were only a few intel-
ligible phrases that I could make out and 'the curse of
Kovi,' repeated over and over again.

"As the moments passed, I found that to understand
his mutterings really didn't matter much to me. I had

become very dizzy, almost to the point of fainting, which had never happened to me before. It was a shaking experience. Lights seemed to flash from behind my eyes. My ears drummed to the sound of his monotone. I didn't collapse but I came very close to it.

"I don't really know how long it went on. When I recovered my senses I found myself sitting across from him on the dirt floor, my legs folded as were his, and strangely conversing with him as if we had known each other a long time.

"He seemed to know why I had come to Haiti, more than I understood myself actually. He knew that I am a professional horseman. How I do not know, even now. Throughout our conversation, his eyes never lost the expression of looking at me as one marked for death; yet there was compassion in his gaze too, as if he sincerely wanted to help me—or perhaps it was that he believed we could gain strength from each other.

"It was shortly thereafter that he dug up a metal canister containing most of the old records and drawings you see on the table. He gave them to me, as if wanting to rid himself of them. Perhaps that was so, for I know now they were responsible for his condition when I found him.

"I stayed with him and, during the hour that followed, the terror seemed to leave his body. When I asked him how this thing had come about, he told me that the curse of *Kovi* was upon him for having used a horse in the tilling of his land. I laughed at this but was stopped short by his shrill warning that I, being a professional horseman and of the family, would suffer the most horrible death of all if something was not done to help me.

"When I heard this and looked more closely at the drawing of *Kovi* in my hands, I felt the greatest fear of my life. I wanted to get away immediately—from Odin, from Haiti, from everything my family represented. But I knew I could not run. It was too late for that. I held the ancient records of my family in my hands. I had nowhere to go but to pursue the legend of *Kovi*. This I knew instinctively and without any doubt, as if I had known always that such a time would come."

The captain paused and Alec remained silent. The captain's world was one he never would understand. He could call it "primitive nonsense," but to the captain it was far more than that.

"I tell you this, Alec, not expecting you to understand but hoping that it will help satisfy your curiosity as to why I am here with Odin. The curse of *Kovi* is upon us."

The captain paused again and no breath seemed to stir within him. "In possessing these ancestral records and drawings," he went on, "I have become involved in what has gone before and, in effect, am held to be an intrinsic part of it. As Fate would have it, I am a horseman not unlike the first of my great ancestors who betrayed his own people to possess a horse. It is my objective to pursue the legend to the end, to *Kovi* himself, if he exists more than in the minds of men, so that I will be freed from the curse of my ancestors."

The captain studied Alec's face, then picked up the papers from the table. "Do I need to tell you, Alec," he said, "that according to these records the home of *Koví* is in this area?"

"You're crazy," Alec said quickly, without thinking.

Surprisingly, no anger showed in the captain's face.

"No, Alec," he said. "I have all the proof I need. He was seen by my people, and it is written in their records. There is the drawing, too, of what they saw. Would you like to see it?"

Without waiting for a reply, the captain picked up one of the drawings and handed it to Alec.

Alec was determined not to recoil at the sight of a weird picture, any more than he had when he saw the grotesque figurine. Each was the work of a superstitious mind, producing what it wanted to see. Yet a feeling of terror swept over him as he looked at the drawing.

He had expected to see a drawing of a supernatural monster, half-man, half-animal, *anything* but the child-like lines that filled the tissue-thin paper. He could make out no central figure. There was just a series of designs, mosaic in composition, depicting eyes and limbs and parts of bodies, some recognizable and others not.

The very air in the room grew cold. The drawing was obviously the work of a person whose imagination was guided by the subconscious.

"What do you see?" the captain asked anxiously. When Alec did not reply, he repeated his question.

It was like looking at a picture puzzle and being asked, *"How many objects can you find? What do you see?"* Alec thought. Only this puzzle conveyed more than one's eyes beheld; it transmitted a cumulative force of *dread* that was almost overpowering. He was seeing it as he was meant to see it, journeying back through time to view the drawing through the eyes and primitive mind of the person who had created it.

"I don't know," he said finally, although in truth he saw many things. An open mouth spoke soundless words to him. A misshapen face that could be part of a horse's head became more terrifying and repulsive as he looked at it. A single dark eye stared back at him from the lower left-hand corner. He recognized a piece of mane and a lone hoof, both seeming to move before his eyes. There were muscleless jaws, open and dripping. There were many more, human and animal and those he did not know. All were hidden within the drawing but easy to find if one wanted to see them.

"*Kovi* exists in many forms," the captain said, his mouth twisting in a smile. "His description has varied from generation to generation."

Alec turned from the drawing to stare blankly at the captain.

"There is a humpbacked hammock just to the southwest of here and, according to the records, that is the home of *Kovi*," the captain continued. "I have been there with Odin during the day. The way is not easy but much of the area has been drained by the new canals and thereby made accessible by foot. That, too, is one of the signs which I cannot ignore."

Alec shuddered, finding it hard to comprehend that the captain believed so strongly in his omens and signs that he would risk his life in pursuing them. His fate, as Alec saw it, lay in his ability not to get lost in the saw-grass wilderness or founder in the black bottomless muck.

"And you believe you will find *Kovi* there?" he asked incredulously.

The captain shrugged his shoulders. "I do not know," he said quietly. "I know only that the signs point that way and I will go."

There was total resignation in the captain's voice and for the first time Alec felt sympathy for him.

"But if *Kovi* is as dangerous as you believe him to be, won't that mean your death too?" he asked. He didn't know if he was humoring the captain or if he really wanted to hear the rest of this incredible story of a man's quest for a supernatural being!

"I cannot believe that I was led all this way to die," the captain said. "If that were true, I would know. But even if I were given such an ominous sign, I would not turn back or change my plans. It is not possible to avoid disaster if it is to come."

Alec turned away, unable to look at the man any longer. He had no doubt that the captain believed every word he said. The captain preferred his bondage to the dark world of mystery and superstition he had believed in since he was a child, as his people had before him. To anyone else the story of *Kovi* was incredible but to the captain it was true. He would pursue his quest until the end.

Alec remained in his seat while the captain gathered up the papers and returned them to the trunk. The end of the captain's search for *Kovi* would come from the natural dangers of the swamp, which punished invaders quickly when mistakes were made.

Alec rose to his feet, wondering if he would be able to break free of the captain's dark world even in the morning. There was no doubt he shared the company of a man not completely sane. There was no other answer to all this, regardless of what sense he had tried to make out of it before.

"If you don't mind, Captain," he said, "I'll go to bed. I'm tired and I want to get an early start in the morning."

The man turned to him, his eyes searching. "Certainly I have no objection," he said kindly. "It has been a long day for you, and I have spoken of too many things that have bewildered you. *Bon soir,* Alec. We will see each other in the morning."

"Good night," Alec said. As tired as he was, he knew it would be a long time before he slept, if sleep came at all. At least he would rest while awaiting the first light of dawn.

9 · Nightmare!

Alec stood before the open window of his second-floor bedroom and stared into the night. It was a beautiful evening with a gigantic span of sky spread before him and a full moon just beginning to rise above the saw grass. To the southwest he could see the high hump-backed outline of a hammock which he believed was the captain's objective, *the home of Kovi*.

Certainly he did not believe any part of such a fan-tastic story! Yet he knew that his own vivid imagination made him very vulnerable to the captain's ramblings.

He turned his mind to other thoughts, knowing he'd get no sleep otherwise. The seemingly endless miles of saw grass glistened beneath the star-spangled sky. He saw many hammocks studding the swamp, like islands in a watery wilderness. He stared at the moon and was conscious of the stillness. Such a world belonged more to night than to day, he decided. It was almost like being alone in the universe.

Here in the Everglades, Nature would forever triumph over Man, regardless of how many drainage ditches were dug. The swamp was vast and confident in its solitude.

Alec wondered why he had been frightened by the swamp during the day but not at night. Perhaps it was the great silence, that and the deep peace that seemed to accompany it. He listened. Any sound would carry miles with bell-like clarity on such a night. But he heard nothing, no shrill cries of distant birds or receding echoes. He was alone, the vast swampland calmly ignoring his presence or, perhaps, accepting him as a friend.

He believed he would be able to sleep. Leaving the window, he went to his bed and stretched out on it, fully clothed. He closed his eyes and kept his thoughts on the great silence outside the window, waiting for sleep to come. It had been a long, hard day and he was very tired.

He didn't know how long he lay there or, actually, whether or not he had slept, when he saw a pair of eyes staring at him in the darkness. They were startlingly cold and dark as obsidian. He believed it was the captain and asked quickly, "What are you doing here?"

He attempted to get up but found he could not rise from the bed. He struggled but could not move. It was then he realized that he must be asleep and dreaming. But a dream never had been so vivid to him before.

He began struggling again and found he was able to wiggle his body across the bed but not rise from it. Nor could he tear his gaze away from the eyes that held him. He believed there was a living presence in the room with him but he did not know whether it was the captain or not. He wanted only to rise and run, yet he could not. And try as he might, he could not wake up to rid himself of the horrible dream.

He opened his mouth but nothing came forth although he shouted as loud as he could. He continued struggling, working his body from one end of the bed to the other in an attempt to rouse himself from his dream. Always the eyes followed him, moving with him, holding him.

He was able to think with a clarity he had not thought possible in a dream. He believed his subconscious was playing tricks on him, recalling in his sleep the captain's unwavering hypnotic stare. He ceased struggling and sought to make out the face behind the eyes. He lay very still.

He stared into the depth of the darkness. An image of terror was vague but there! He made out a misshapen head with no distinguishable features, known yet unknown. He believed that the horror which had seemed a dream was not a dream but *reality!* The thought brought superhuman strength to his limbs and he tried to break the invisible bonds that held him to the bed while the misshapen head hovered directly above him.

His lips moved but no sound came. A sweet, sickening odor filled his nostrils. He threw back his head, gasping from the overpowering scent and his efforts to break away. He twisted, squirmed, seeking escape.

Madness possessed him and he found that he had the strength to heave his body forward. His eyes bulged in their sockets as he sought to raise his hands from the bedsheets to strike back at whatever was above him. He succeeded in lifting his hands and, fighting for breath, tried to protect himself. Words poured forth from his lips for the first time. He did not know what he was saying, nor did he recognize his voice, which was distorted and unnatural. His hands sought to seize the fleshless face!

Suddenly, as if he had broken through a ghostly barrier, he was wide-awake. The bedsheets were wringing wet and his breath came in great gasps as he gulped air into his lungs. He was alone in the room. The moonlight made it bright enough to enable him to see that no one was there.

He went to the washbasin and doused his head in cold water. There had been nothing, he told himself savagely.

It had been a dream, prompted by the stories of a man who believed in the supernatural. He had succumbed to them in his sleep, his own imagination giving way to what he had been told. It was an experience he never wanted to go through again.

Everyone dreamed, he told himself, *and this one had been a nightmare to end all nightmares.*

The room darkened as a cloud passed beneath the moon. He went to the window and looked out across the saw grass. A chill swept over him which he attributed to the sudden cooling of the night and not to his fear. The moon emerged and once more the room was filled with ghostly light.

There was nothing to fear from a dream, even a nightmare, he told himself. Yet his heart continued thudding against his chest as he attempted to bring order to his thoughts.

Judging by the height of the moon, he had been asleep all of two hours. He had seen the frightening image in his dream because of the captain's story of *Kovi* and the horrible drawing. It made little difference whether or not he believed in *Kovi* he told himself. Known or unknown, real or not real, *the monster now lived in his subconscious.*

Alec's heart thudded faster as he accepted this fact. He remained at the window, not wanting to go to bed lest he dream again. He wondered if it were possible to die of fear caused by a dream. Quickly, he rid himself of such a thought by dousing his head in water again. He would remain awake the rest of the night. Tomorrow and during the days that followed, when normal life resumed, he would forget *Kovi*. It would be as if this night had never been.

Meanwhile he sought inner peace and comfort from the tranquillity of the swamp. The skies were clear and for a long while Alec listened to the stillness of the night. He felt absolutely alone in the world. There came to him the gentle sound of a breeze stirring the palm fronds and water.

His heart resumed its normal beat. Taut muscles relaxed. He responded to his freedom from the nightmare by walking across the room and back. Suddenly he came to a stop before the window again, every sense alert.

He had heard a sound outside. It was not the lapping of the water or the stirring of a palm frond. It was the soft stealth of moving feet, not those of an animal but a man!

His keen eyes searched the darkness for movement that would betray another's presence. A moment passed, then a black silhouette stepped around the corner of the house into the moonlight. The figure stood still, legs astride. Was it Odin returning from the Indian village? But the silhouette was too large and tall for him, more the size of the captain, Alec decided.

He waited for the figure to move, hoping the man would pass beneath his window so he might see him better. Finally the figure strode silently by and Alec had no trouble recognizing the captain.

Alec stepped back from the window. He had no intention of leaving the room. He cared nothing about what the captain did at night; it was no concern of his. The captain might well be off to his eternal quest of *Kovi*. It made no difference. He would remain in the bedroom until dawn.

It was only as the moments passed that Alec's resolution wavered. He wondered if he might not be doing exactly what the captain had planned. What if the captain's story of *Kovi* had been only a hoax to frighten him into keeping to his room, asleep or not? The captain coveted the Black for his mare. Perhaps he had no intention of waiting until the end of the racing season to breed his mare as had been agreed, not when he had the opportunity to do it *now!*

Distant, muffled snorts reached Alec's ears and he went quickly to the door, his decision made. A cold anger swept over him as he ran down the stairs. The captain took what he wanted; he was as remorseless as he was powerful; he would stop at nothing to breed his mare to the Black!

Alec opened the front door and sped down the porch steps into the night. He ran across the yard, knowing what he had to do. No hands would touch the Black but his own. This he would fight for, regardless of the odds against him.

There was no caution to his movements as he approached the barn. He heard the Black's shrill neigh, meant clearly for the mare, and he knew he was too late.

10 · The Fight

Alec stopped at the barn. They were behind it and not far away. At first he was aware only of the beauty of the blending of the horses' bodies, coal-black and silver-gray. They were a tableau in the shimmering light of the moon. The mare was tied to the fence and stood absolutely still, almost as if frozen by the arrogance of the Black who was alongside her, his tail held high and neck arched mightily. His small head was thrust out to hers and she squealed excitedly in answer to his panting snorts. He bit her lightly on the neck and, when she retaliated by striking out at him with her hind legs, he skillfully jumped away, then immediately closed in on her again.

It was a game he knew well, one of a mare testing his strength before final acquiescence.

Only then did Alec become fully aware of the captain and what he was doing. He had the Black by the long shank chain and was attempting to curb the stallion's excitement by yanking it repeatedly. He shouted something in French at the top of his voice. Then, as if suddenly realizing his commands were not in the language the stallion understood, he shouted in English, *"Back! When I say back, you back!"*

The stallion screamed in rage and pain but continued to ignore the man for the waiting mare. His consuming interest was in her despite the captain's efforts. He plunged toward her again and bit her more threateningly, low on the neck and in front of the withers. He held on to her this time, whirling her around again and again until she stood quietly before him. He could be as rough as required, but gentle as well. He began licking her wounds.

Suddenly, the sharp, agonizing pain in his mouth was more than he could bear. He went back on his hind legs, seeking relief.

Alec ran across the clearing, knowing the captain had the shank chain under the stallion's lips and across his gums, the snap attached to the halter ring on the far side. If he didn't stop the captain, the Black in his pain and frenzy would kill him!

The stallion had turned his attention from the mare to strike savagely at the man who was causing him so much pain. But the captain moved fast, escaping the intended blow; then he began using the powerful leverage in his hands to its utmost. Repeatedly, he pulled down the shank with all his strength. The Black went back on his haunches in an effort to escape the pain of the chain cutting viciously into his gums.

"*Assez! Ça suffit!* Enough!" the captain screamed at the stallion while backing him with terrible force. "You are a devil! You do not treat her this way! You go forward when I say you do, not before!" Relentlessly he jerked downward on the shank until the Black was almost falling over himself in an attempt to get away.

Alec's headlong rush brought him up behind the captain. He hurled himself upon the man's back, seeking to pin his arms to his side and prevent him from using the shank. For a few seconds he held on, his onslaught coming as a complete surprise to the captain. He sought to topple the great body clasped in his arms by throwing his own weight to one side as leverage. He managed to bring the captain to one knee, but suddenly the man straightened and swung upward and back with all his strength.

Alec knew immediately that he was no match for this man in deadly combat. He was hurled to one side and around. He held on to the bulging neck while being whirled like a pinwheel; then a large hand caught him by the shoulder and the other hand, clenched into a fist, smashed against the side of his head. He fell hard upon the ground.

Instantly there was the taste of blood in his mouth. He didn't quite lose consciousness for he could hear shouts from the captain and squeals from the Black. The blood seemed never-ending and he choked upon it.

Dazedly he found himself wondering if one could drown in his own blood.

He fought to maintain consciousness. His vision was blurred but he could make out the captain's figure as the man sought to regain control of the Black. The stallion was plunging toward him, squealing and pawing.

The captain avoided the flying hoofs and tried to stop the horse. He jerked on the shank chain but his move came an instant too late. The horse rose above him, standing straight up on his hind legs. The captain dodged quickly to one side, avoiding the striking forelegs again, but only by a few scant inches. His fear mounted. He pulled forcefully on the shank, trying to knock the stallion off balance. He was in time, for the horse screamed in pain. Confident that he had won, the captain yanked harder to bring the pawing forelegs to the ground.

The black stallion moved quickly, walking on his hind legs while his forelegs continued to strike. The captain backed off, suddenly terrified by the plunging horse who would not be beaten despite all he could do! Dropping the lead shank, he screamed a torrent of French and ran for the safety of the barn.

A moment later, the Black moved to Alec's prone figure, his head lowered to it. His blown-out nostrils sniffed the blood and he shied clear, uncertain and troubled.

Alec tried to speak to his horse but his head was throbbing with pain and the blood that filled his throat caused a choking nausea. He was unable to utter a word, even a whisper. He tried to clear his throat but his efforts only caused the growing blackness to envelop him all the more. He lay still again, not wanting to lose total consciousness.

As if in a dream, he saw the Black return to the mare. Again their bodies blended into one. He could hear her sharp squeals and the lashing of her hoofs. There was a quick whirling of their bodies and then, suddenly, the night became still. He could hear nothing, see nothing. The blackness was complete. Alec had lost consciousness.

The captain searched the barn looking for any weapons he might use against the stallion. A leather riding whip hung on a peg in the entryway. He took it. He had forgotten where he'd left the long-handled pitchfork, and it was several minutes before he finally found it. He was determined to protect his mare as well as himself from the onslaught of the most savage horse he had ever come across. He had judged wrong; this was no horse to be bred to his mare. The black stud was the devil himself!

Yet he did not leave the barn immediately with his weapons. For the first time in his life he was deathly afraid of a horse. He stood in the doorway where he could see the stallion whirling his mare around, dominating her, bringing her to her knees until, finally, she stood quietly before him. His heart went out to her but he could do nothing.

Moments later, when the stallion whinnied and left the mare, the captain stole silently forward, the pitchfork extended. He saw the stallion return to where Alec lay on the ground and for a fleeting second he wondered if the youth was dead. He hadn't meant to strike him so hard. It was the horror of the moment, at finding his arms pinned from behind while the stallion came at him.

The Black sniffed the blood on Alec and shied away again. The one person who might have soothed him lay still. Suddenly, a new kind of terror possessed him, one of great aloneness he had long forgotten. He drew back, startled and uncertain. A figure loomed in the night and he turned upon it.

Savagely, he attacked but backed off immediately when the steel prongs of the pitchfork pierced his chest and he felt deep, agonizing pain. He sought escape, his natural instincts telling him to run to survive. The sharp prongs of the pitchfork were thrust at him again.

He whirled and ran, gaining full stride almost immediately. His mane and tail swept in the wind he created, while the lead shank trailed at his side. Fear and pain had awakened within him the memory of another life apart from the one he had lived these past years. His body responded quickly to the challenge of surviving alone by taking him toward the swamp and escape!

11 · The Grassy Sea

"Alec," the captain pleaded, kneeling beside the youth, *"Je vous en prie . . ."* He spoke in French as if English was unknown to him, then, "I beg you . . ."

With difficulty Alec opened his eyes and listened to him.

". . . forgive me. I did not mean to hurt you."

There was apology and sympathy in the captain's words but not in his eyes. Alec wiped the blood from his mouth and gathered what strength he had left; then he kicked upward with all his might. He felt the impact as his feet struck the captain in the chest, tumbling him over backwards.

Breathing hard from his effort, he staggered to his feet and threw himself upon the captain, his hands reaching for the man's face. Once more he learned quickly that he was no match physically for the captain. He was thrown off and pinned to the ground.

The blow Alec expected didn't come. Instead he was pulled firmly but kindly to his feet and made to walk. He was aware of nothing but the sound of the breeze in the palm trees and, a little later, the lapping of water. He shook his head, trying to clear his vision, to see where the captain had taken him.

They stood at the edge of the swamp, the house behind them.

"Where is my horse?" he pleaded. "What have you done to him?"

"He ran off. I could not stop him." The captain would not meet Alec's gaze. "I tried but I could not stop him," he repeated.

The dark skin was drawn tight across the captain's face; there was a tenseness that Alec had not seen before. He knew the man had been terrified and badly beaten by the Black. It was no consolation to him now.

"He went this way?" Alec felt his heart sink as he looked down the vein of black water that laced the saw grass before him. The bank on either side of the channel was dry from drought and drainage. He had no need to wait for the captain's reply, for in the bright moonlight he could see the plowing of the Black's hoofs in the muck.

Alec tried to control the wild pounding of his blood that only increased the throbbing in his head. What kind of frenzy had driven the Black into the vastness of the swamp?

The captain shrugged his shoulders. "It was his most direct route of . . ."

"Escape," Alec finished bitterly. "What did you do to him after he bred your mare? That was what you wanted, wasn't it? You planned it from the beginning. You had no intention of waiting."

The captain turned away, and there was a moment of absolute quiet between them. Alec realized it would serve no purpose to find out why the Black had sought frenzied escape from the captain. The horrible shock was that he had chosen the swamp as his refuge, and the odds were great that he would not survive the night. There was no sound from the swamp, no sign of life except for a multitude of insects. Yet Alec knew there was an ominous massing of forces between him and his horse. His fear for the Black's life was not from unknown dangers but from those that were very real. He was not going to lose the Black to alligators, snakes or bogs!

"*Oui*, Alec," the captain said finally. "It is as you say, I could not wait. I regret it now as much as you do."

The moon disappeared behind thin, filmy clouds and the swamp became more dark and silent, the tall reeds and bushes looking like shadowy figures in the night. It was as if a dark curtain had been dropped over this strange, terrifying land.

"It's too late for regret," Alec said. "I *must* find him."

"You have no choice but to wait here," the captain answered. "He will return very soon."

"He won't come back if the swamp claims him first," Alec said. "I can't take that chance." He turned his gaze from the gleam of dark water to the deep hoofprints on the bank. "How far could he go before becoming bogged down?"

The captain stared blankly at him, hesitated, then said, "He could go a long way *but he won't*. We must wait for him to return. We have no choice."

The clouds passed and the full brightness of the moon was upon them again; the swamp emerged in all its grimness, swelling and triumphant before Alec's eyes.

"*I* have a choice," he said. "If he knows I'm near, he'll come to me. Will you help me?"

The deep quiet held them while Alec repeated, "Will you help me find him? *It was your doing,*" he added accusingly, yet there was no anger in his voice, only a plea for assistance.

The captain shuddered and said nothing. The dark water washed about the reeds nearby and, in the far distance, Alec heard the strange cry of a bird. It jogged his memory, as if he had heard it before—a faded, shadowy, half-conscious recollection. He dismissed it quickly from his mind.

"Are you going with me or not?" he asked again. "You said he would not have gone far."

The captain seemed to be thinking hard as if he didn't know what to do next. Finally he came to a decision and said kindly, "Please, Alec, it was my doing, as you say, but you must wait until morning. If he has not returned by then, I will search for him with you. You must believe me. It is no place to go at night."

"It may be too late by morning," Alec answered quickly. He realized that it was the captain's superstitious beliefs that kept him from the swamp at night. The story of *Kovi* might have been told to frighten him and keep him in his room, as he suspected, but there was no doubt in Alec's mind that the captain believed every word of it.

He moved down the path beside the black water while the captain screamed after him, "Please . . . I tell you not to go, Alec. . . . *Je vous en prie* . . . you must wait. . . ."

Alec neither stopped nor turned. He did not want to meet the captain's eyes that begged so desperately for belief. He knew they moved him; he could ignore such things as old drawings and documents, legends and figurines, even voices, but he could not ignore what lay in the captain's eyes. They nakedly revealed his innermost thoughts. The captain truly believed that to go into the swamp at night meant certain death—not from natural enemies but *imaginary* ones. He feared the supernatural monster he called *Kovi*.

Alec walked along the bank, finding the mud firmer beneath his weight than he had thought it would be. With secure footing he would be able to move fast.

"You will die with your horse!" the captain shouted. "It is your last chance, Alec . . . your last chance!"

Alec was shaken by the warning, but he didn't turn back. An unending maze of wasteland stretched before him. He had needed the captain's help. Despite his distrust, even horror at what the captain had done, he found that he no longer felt any anger or fear of him, only sympathy for a mind deranged.

He slipped, regained his footing, and hurried on. His one hope was that the Black had not gone far and that he would find him soon, at any turn of the channel. The severe pain in his head had subsided but his vision was still blurred. It was, he realized, as if he moved forward in a dream, not totally unlike the one he'd had earlier that night. To prove to himself that he was not dreaming this time, he took hold of a saw-grass spear and pressed the sharp barbs into his flesh until blood came. Then he went on.

His steps became more cautious as he continued along the channel with its thin vein of black water in the middle. He stayed high on the bank, following his horse's hoofprints.

He refused to think of turning back. Regardless of what he faced, he had made his decision to go on. He forced fear from his mind. He would be cautious but unafraid; that way he might avoid all natural dangers and traps.

He could no longer see the hammock behind him; the saw-grass empire was all around him. He wondered if he'd be able to retrace his steps when the time came to return. One could easily get lost in this wilderness.

He continued on, slipping down the bank and into the water occasionally but for the most part making good time. He was startled by a metallic sound nearby and came to an abrupt stop. It was only the whisper of the tall grass as the night breeze freshened. He paused to listen to it, so he would fix it in his mind and not be startled by it again. It was necessary that his imagination play no tricks on him in the swamp. His search for his horse was a gamble, requiring nerve and caution. Imagination had no place here.

It was a simple matter to stay on course. He had only to follow the waterway and the Black's hoofprints. He forced quiet on his limbs and brain and was determined not to let any strange sounds frighten him. Fear that might cause panic was his greatest danger. If he kept calm and faced natural dangers cautiously but unafraid, he would find his horse and return safely with him. He must have self-confidence in his ability to see it through. There was no turning back. The game had begun and the stakes were high, higher than they had ever been in his life.

He estimated that he had gone another mile when the saw-grass wall on his right gave way to form a large cove in which apparently the water had receded months ago. The crusted mud beneath his feet was baked hard by daily exposure to a relentless sun.

The cove was all of fifty yards deep and Alec searched everywhere for prints left by his horse. He found nothing. He had lost the Black's trail!

The saw grass standing around the cove was dead, the life-giving water having been drained from its roots long ago. Running into the cove were many dry, narrow channels and Alec realized his horse could have taken any one of them. He had a sickening moment in which he accepted defeat; without a trail to follow, he had reached the end of his search. Then, quickly, he shook off his anguish and went to each of the channels, seeking prints or broken stalks that might show him the way.

Again he found nothing. He began whistling and shouting, calling to his horse. When, finally, his calls ended, no answering neigh came from the swamp.

He decided to stay where he was and call to his horse time and time again. He should not go down any of the dry waterways unless it was the right one; otherwise he might find himself in a maze with no hope of finding the Black or getting out himself. He must rest and conserve his energy for the time being. If the Black answered, he would hear him.

For several moments the night was deathly still, then he heard the lapping of water against the stalks of saw grass. It was louder than the breeze could have caused. An alligator? He concentrated on the dark water of the main channel, watching for the slightest ripple.

He saw a figure emerge from the channel, feet slipping as it climbed the bank. Then a black silhouette stood between him and the moon.

Once over the shock at seeing the captain, Alec called, "Over here!"

He wondered what had caused the man to change his mind and follow. The air was as still as in a dream and for a fleeting second Alec felt apprehension rise within him. Might not the greatest danger of all be from the captain himself, with his supernatural beliefs that could panic both of them?

He cast aside his doubts as the black figure strode up to him. The captain would help him find his horse, for he knew the swamp.

There was no emotion in the captain's eyes. He simply stared at Alec. His face was no longer strong but pinched and haggard, as old as time. He might have control of his body, Alec decided, but he had by no means conquered his fears. It was as if, once his decision had been made to enter the swamp, he had plunged recklessly to his own doom. His eyes were touched with death, those of a man observing his own funeral.

Alec felt a chill sweep over him. "I can't find his trail anywhere," he said, hoping to penetrate to the mind of the professional horseman behind that fearful stare. "Do you know which way he might have gone?"

The captain smiled faintly, as if he found something humorous in Alec's words. Finally he answered, "All the channels lead to the same place."

Alec found it even more difficult to cope with the captain's smile. He made an attempt to bring order and sanity into his search for the Black.

"To where?"

"*To the home of Kovi,*" the captain replied. Despite his smile, Alec knew the captain was terrified almost to the point of immobility.

Alec moved off toward the nearest dry waterway, but stopped when he heard the captain screaming at him, "No, no . . . *la route vite!*" Then it was repeated over and over again. *"La route vite!"*

Alec had sufficient knowledge of French to understand, and he turned back. But where was the short route?

The captain headed for a waterway on the far edge of the cove, and Alec followed him without a word. It was the last channel he would have selected had he been alone. Despite the captain's terror, Alec decided he would be able to use his knowledge of the swamp. He hurried along, believing he could cope with what had to be done.

The stench of rotting vegetation assailed his nostrils as he followed the captain deeper into the yellow, dried-out saw grass. He tried not to breathe it in. Then, from afar, he heard the strange cry from the bird he had heard before. He listened to it and it seemed to be coming closer! He glanced up at the night sky but saw no sign of the bird, only heard it's never-ending cry. Then with electrifying suddenness it seemed to be directly over-head.

He stopped, his feet frozen in place. The captain had halted, too, and Alec looked questioningly at him. But the man was of no help. He seemed to have turned to stone while staring into the sky overhead.

The cry never ceased and the night was filled with its echoes and re-echoes, as if the intention of the bird was to awaken all the inhabitants of the swamp. Alec felt the first wave of terror sweep over him. He knew he was on the verge of panic and sought desperately to control it.

The source of the cry was a night bird, he told himself, nothing else. It was a bird he could not name but a bird nevertheless. It was nothing to be alarmed about. He would not be subject to superstitious terror, as was the captain. Yet, as he continued listening to the cries which were so much like the haunting, piping flute notes of the captain's music, his stomach turned over in mounting panic. What possessed him? What was real? What was imagined?

Finally the cry ended as suddenly as it had begun. They stood dazedly in the great silence of the swamp. Alec turned to the captain. The man's eyes were closed. Alec continued watching him, hoping for a rational explanation of the strange frightening cry. But he realized he would get no answer from the captain. The cry had paralyzed the man with fear. He was whimpering like an animal. Alec waited quietly for a long while for his terror to subside.

When, finally, the captain moved, Alec expected him to go back the way they had come. Instead, he began running up the dry waterway, leaving Alec behind!

Alec stumbled as he followed, and fell into the saw grass. He felt the lash of the sharp-bladed stalks and cried out in pain; quickly, he regained his feet and set out to catch up to the dark figure running up the slough.

The night remained quiet but Alec no longer felt that he and the captain were alone. On either side of the waterway there seemed to be a gathering of grotesque and fantastic shapes. *"Only bushes and grass!"* he told himself. *"Keep your mind on what has to be done!"* But strange omens persisted in his mind; he ran faster, hoping to rid himself of them.

The bank became steep and he saw the first gleam of dark water in the center of the channel. They must be nearing a spring or the hammock itself! He followed the captain down the bank, wading through the water to the other side. He watched where he stepped and looked for any ripples in the water that would warn him of alligators and snakes.

Turning a dog-leg in the slough, he followed the captain through the shallows again, pulling his feet free of the muck as he climbed the bank. On top, immense tongues of saw grass rose above his head. It would be easy to lose all sense of direction here and he wondered if he'd ever be able to find his way out. He pushed on.

The muck beneath his feet became powder-dry and he made good time. Yet he could not catch up to the captain who was running all-out ahead of him. Soon, Alec knew, the channel must come to an end and the hammock would rise above the screen of saw grass. As forbidding as it might be, he would welcome it. He ran faster to catch up to the captain.

The slough widened with dramatic suddenness. At the end of it, the hammock rose majestically from the grassy sea. A wall of palm trees and live oaks stood at the water's edge, but above and behind the trees Alec saw the grim outline of the hammock's spine thrust up against the moonlit sky.

The captain came to a halt and looked back for the first time, as if to find out if Alec was still there. His dark eyes shone in the night, and he waved his arms crazily, pointing toward the hammock. He screamed a torrent of French or Haitian words or a language Alec could not understand, but it made no difference.

Alec knew the meaning of the words. The captain was telling him that they had reached *the home of Kovi*.

12 · The Home of Koví

The ground became spongy beneath Alec's feet as he followed the captain into a long wallow. He heard the cough of a bull alligator somewhere in the dark but he knew his greatest danger was stepping into a sinkhole. One false step and, without the captain's help, he'd be sucked deep into the black embrace of the viscous mud.

The captain stayed on the bank wherever possible, grasping roots that were anchored in solid ground to pull himself along. Alec followed closely, staring into the darkness and feeling very much alone; he knew his horse never would have traveled such a route as this.

He saw the glint of moonlight on slime-green water

just ahead. It was a backwater rather than a spring; a low point in the swamp, a stagnant pool without current, awaiting the summer rains to bring it back to life.

The powerful stench from the rotted tangle of grass and plants invaded his senses again. He staggered from the effect of it and from his weariness as well. His footsteps squished in mud and water that had spilled into the slough from the stagnant bayou.

They moved slowly toward what looked like a solid wall of twisted branches and tree roots fighting the encroachment of the swamp. He followed the captain out of the slough and once more the ground became firm, a deep mat of moss, beneath his feet.

The captain's strides quickened as he drove through the heavy growth, hunching over to enter a dense tangle of thickets and vines. Alec lessened the distance between them, his smaller size making it easier for him to move beneath the jungle canopy overhead.

Upon reaching the high ground of the hammock, the captain came to a stop and turned to Alec. In the bizarre light, his features appeared more Indian than Negroid.

Alec said, "My horse could not have come this way."

"If he did not turn back, we will find him on the other side of the hammock," the captain answered, his voice but a whisper. "The source of all the other channels begins in a large spring there."

Once more the captain was on his way, snaking through the heavy growth. Alec hurried after him until, finally, they reached a clearing, and the hammock's spine rose above them.

The captain encircled the base of the hill which,

Alec knew, was an Indian burial-mound. There were no hills other than those made by man in the swamp. This one was over fifty feet high and covered with lank grass and palmetto bushes. Its soil was composed of the bones and skulls of Indian dead and their enemies. The inaccessibility of this hammock had provided the Indians with a secure hideaway from all who sought them. Alec didn't want to think of what it offered him now.

Farther on, the captain came to another stop. He caught Alec's arm and pulled him around roughly. "Not a sound," he whispered urgently. "Listen."

Alec heard a horrible faint sound close by. He turned quickly in the direction from which it had come. A large gray figure passed between him and the silent bushes below. It melted so quickly into the blackness that he couldn't be sure what it was—or, a moment later, if it had been anything at all.

He turned to the captain but the man wouldn't meet his gaze. "What was it?" he asked.

The captain ignored his question and began running again. Alec followed, telling himself that he had seen nothing that couldn't be explained. He would *not* be frightened.

He slipped to his knees but got up to hurry after the captain through a dense growth of high ferns. Shut in as they were, he understood how the world could seem changed for anyone in such a place. The wind was hushed but he heard the murmur of the great swamp beyond, and he wondered what, besides themselves, moved within the heavy veils of darkness.

A sudden cry broke the silence, swelling to the heavens and seemingly triumphant. A shiver ran down his back and his strides slowed immediately. What could it be—a catbird, a night owl, or what?

Ahead, the captain was running as fast as before. Alec hurried after him. He must hold onto the captain as long as he could; it was better, much better, that he did not travel alone. How much farther did they have to go?

Finally they reached a deep basin only partially filled with black water. This was the spring, the source of the other channels. The captain said, "He will come here if he has not already turned back. Be still," he added in warning.

Alec wondered how long the captain would be able to control his fear of whatever it was he believed threatened them. His gaze was not toward any of the dry sloughs through which the Black might come, but on the dense foliage beside the black pool. Alec would have liked to be able to look out from inside the captain's mind, to know what it was for which he searched.

For several minutes Alec listened for the sound of the Black's hoofs. He heard nothing but the soft lapping of water in the pool. Then came a sound unlike any he had heard before. It became more distinct, a soft murmur, almost a whimper that he immediately associated with an injured animal!

His eyes searched the edge of the swamp from which the sound had come. High in a group of cabbage palms he saw a movement, a gleam of white between the fronds —then, as quickly, it was gone.

Alec felt fear rise within him. He sought to subdue it by angrily accusing himself of weakness. He would not be led into the captain's superstitious world of obscure shadows and ominous sounds. He had seen nothing ghostly or unreal but some kind of animal! He allowed his cold anger to come forth in all its fury, hoping to freeze out his fear.

Finally he turned to the captain and found him staring high into the trees as if whatever had made the cry was still clearly visible to him. Looking into those fearful dark eyes, Alec knew without doubt that the captain believed he faced certain death.

Suddenly there was a great shaking of the captain's body, as if he was making an attempt to overcome whatever horror and fear possessed him. Alec put a hand on his arm but the captain brushed it roughly to one side. Then, quickly, he walked toward the trees, his back straight, like someone who had never known the meaning of fear.

Alec watched the captain disappear among the cabbage palms and wondered momentarily if the fear he had seen in the man's eyes was only a reflection of his own. Perhaps, like the captain, he was beginning to exaggerate everything out of proportion to the truth. If he lost control of himself, he would know panic and terror.

Alec forced himself to wait quietly for the captain's return. He concentrated on the brilliance of the moon reflected in the black water. He would not let the captain or the overwhelming solitude of the swamp break him down! His gaze turned to a tall oak tree near the grove of cabbage palms. Perhaps if he climbed it he might be able to see his horse approaching the hammock.

A hunched figure darted from the bushes and staggered toward him. At first Alec didn't believe it was the captain, for the figure was neither tall nor long-limbed but horribly bent and moving forward feebly, head hanging close to the ground and eyes lowered. Alec shuddered and ran forward.

"What happened?" But it was almost as if he were talking to a ghost. He attempted to hold up the captain but his great bulk was too much for him and the man slipped to the ground. Alec looked into a face he barely recognized.

It was gaunt, sallow and pinched; the dark skin, more gray than black, was drawn so tightly about the cheekbones that they seemed ready to burst the flesh that held them. Instinctively, Alec shrank back in horror and confusion at the physical change in a man who, for all his beliefs, had possessed immense strength.

Again he asked, "What happened to you?"

The haunted eyes were open and staring. The thick lips moved and the tongue slid from side to side but no words came, only stuttering, stammering sounds.

Alec held the captain's head for a long while, waiting for sounds to become words while the mouth kept opening and shutting like a fish's.

What had the captain seen or done in a few minutes' time to cause such great horror? he wondered.

Alec could feel his skin drawing tightly over his bones. The captain's mouth finally stopped opening and closing but the lifeless eyes remained on him, never blinking, never leaving him for a second.

Alec knew he was close to panic. He sought control in angry self-accusation of weakness. He told himself furiously that he had nothing to fear, even now. Whatever the captain had seen had been through the eyes and mind of a demented person. It would not be the same for him. He did not believe in *Kovi* or any other supernatural monster. He would not let his mind be influenced by someone of a superstitious race. He had only the natural dangers of the swamp to face. He must think of it as nothing else!

"Can you hear me?" Alec asked the captain as if speaking to a child.

With great effort, the captain raised the upper part of his body until he was in a seated position; then he began rocking slightly back and forth while his dark, staring eyes remained on Alec.

"Will you get up?" Alec asked, trying to lift him to his feet. The captain pushed him away and remained where he was, his black hair falling over his face; his rocking continued.

He would never be able to move him, Alec decided. He had no doubt that the captain believed he had seen *Kovi*. Nothing else could account for such terror and deterioration of his physical and mental capabilities. The captain was suffering an adventure of horror the like of which Alec could only imagine. He must not visualize what it was or he, too, would live in the captain's nightmare.

"I must go for help. Do you hear me? Do you understand?" he pleaded.

Alec waited for a nod of the head, anything that might give him some assurance the captain understood. Instead, the man smiled faintly. Alec fought back the panic that came to him quickly at sight of that grim smile; it seemed to imply that the captain knew all about where he was going and what would happen to him.

Alec shuddered and rose to his feet. He must find his horse quickly and then ride for help. It was the only possible, sensible, sane solution to what he faced.

"Stay here," he said quietly, "and I'll be back as soon as I can. It may take a long time but wait." He didn't know if the captain understood him or not; it didn't matter any more.

Alec walked quickly past the pool. Somewhere in the darkness he heard a single strident note, followed by a rippling movement in the water. An alligator was there, waiting for him, but he had no intention of wading through the water to reach the slough on the other side. He intended to skirt the pool along the edges, but first he must climb the tall oak tree to see if he could sight his horse.

As he neared the grove of cabbage palms, he heard a rustling in the fronds. "A bird or an animal," he decided, "anything but what I'm thinking. Keep going."

He went on, keeping to the watery edge of the grove, and placing each foot carefully before him so as not to step on anything that might be lying in wait. The full moon helped him find his way and he glanced at it often, dreading the clouds in its path which hid its light from time to time.

Suddenly there was a crackling noise from a nearby clump of palmetto bushes. He froze, waiting in the absolute silence that followed. He saw nothing, and decided he had disturbed an animal, anything but what his nerves and imagination would have him believe. He told himself again that he had nothing to fear except what he created in his own mind.

He went on, cautiously making his way around trees and mangroves. Once again, a sudden noise startled him and he came to a stop. This time, it was the low piping note he had come to know so well. He felt his heart beat faster.

Several minutes passed before he heard it again, this time coming from another direction. "It has to be a night bird," he told himself. "Keep going." It was repeated several more times before dying in the night.

He walked very fast, never looking for the source of the sound. For all he knew, his ears were playing tricks on him. But the low note came again, from far behind. He did not turn to look back but kept walking, faster still. The note came closer, rising in intensity until it became a horrible whistle. Still Alec did not look back. He would have liked to believe it was all nonsense but it wasn't. His discomfort grew as he continued on his way. His face twitched; he ground his teeth, grimly determined to keep going and not look back. What was real and what was imagined?

The whistling continued and now seemed to come from all about him. He stopped abruptly and clapped his hands over his ears. His eyes searched the trees. There was nothing, just as he'd expected, *nothing at all.*

What then accounted for the noise? It resounded from everywhere, swelling and triumphant, insistent, surging and falling, coming from afar and yet near, as if drawing him, luring him—to what?

Was this what had terrified the captain? Was it a cry of madness, created in the captain's mind and now in his own?

Alec let his hands drop to his sides. "I hear nothing," he said aloud, "nothing at all." Would his mind accept his words, his determination to go on?

He ran forward, pushing the long ghostly veils of Spanish moss out of his way. When he reached the trunk of the tall oak tree, he realized that the night had become hushed again, as if the noise had never been. Perhaps this was so, he decided. What nasty twist of the mind had made it seem so real? He must look at it no other way if he was to survive this night of terror.

His gaze traveled up the trunk of the tree with its strong boughs laden with Spanish moss. It rose well above the nearby cabbage palms, and from the top he'd be able to see far into the swamp.

Springing up, he caught hold of the lowest limb, and pulled himself to the first crotch of the tree. From there he moved quickly, from limb to limb, higher and higher. And during his climbing, which was so normal and familiar to him, he believed that his own world was the true world, one in which everything was visible and tangible. Anything else was false and he would continue to deny it.

He reached the uppermost limbs of the oak tree and had no trouble seeing over the tufted heads of the cabbage palms. The limb swayed beneath his weight, but he had no fear of its breaking. His gaze scanned the sea of saw grass spread before him, and he waited impatiently for the moon to emerge from behind a filmy bank of clouds.

Finally, he was able to make out the rambling courses of the dry sloughs running through the saw grass. His eyes followed each one until they became fixed on a single moving object. He shouted at the top of his voice, his call to the Black filling the night.

13 · Koví

The black stallion was nearing the end of the dry slough when he came to a sudden stop. He stood silhouetted in the moonlight, as if turned to stone.

Alec did not call to him again but started down the tree. He was halfway to the ground when he heard the animal-like whimpering. It came with electrifying suddenness and he froze immediately, his hands clutching the trunk of the tree to keep from falling. He was certain it had come from high in the branches overhead. What animals could climb trees—raccoons, opossums?

The whimpering echoed faintly at first, then grew in intensity until it shook the area with a pathetic sobbing.

There was a primitive timbre to the sound, and Alec realized that no animal could make such a human sound.

Was it real? Was it imagined? he asked himself once more. Was his mind playing tricks on him again? He stared into the darkness, and knew he was becoming dreadfully frightened. *He could hear the whimpering whether it was imaginary or not!*

Suddenly it stopped and there was a long silence. Alec made up his mind to get to the ground, to run, hoping to reach his horse and find courage in the Black's company.

He slid down the trunk, his feet reaching for a lower limb. Above him in the leafy branches he saw a movement. He clutched the tree, his eyes riveted to a dim figure. Real or not, it stood out in the darkness. It was no animal but an impression of fleeting whiteness . . . or a beam of light . . . not strong but misty and with grotesque human features! Then it was gone and the whimpering came again, a new sound, higher than before and more sorrowful, sobbing as if its origin was in the very depths of despair.

The pathetic sobbing and the figure he had seen in the branches above shocked Alec into panic. Instinctively, his hands let go of the trunk and he fell, clutching boughs to slow down his momentum but frantically seeking escape from what he believed was following him and blocking out the sky.

He struck the ground hard, rolled over, and clambered to his feet. Then he ran into the brush as fast as he could go, without ever once looking behind. All reasoning, all reality had given way before the grotesque form he had seen in the branches. It was a terror he had never known before.

He plunged through trees and crossed stretches of deep muck and black water, not caring what dangers lay in wait. Nothing could be compared to the horror that was behind him! All else was hidden from his eyes. He wanted only to melt away in the darkness so he could not be found. He plunged into the swamp, not feeling the saw-grass barbs that ripped open his flesh. He believed there was no escape for he heard the mournful whimpering in every direction he ran.

The wave of terror that possessed him was never-ending. He did not stop running even though he believed every path led to his destruction. He ran until he could go no farther and then kept on. A frantic dash carried him out of the saw grass into a dry slough. He slipped and fell and didn't get up. He lay there, waiting for his breath to return and wondering if the horrible whimpering would ever stop.

Finally he struggled to his feet and began running again. The faster he ran, the more he was pursued by terror. His headlong flight without thought of what lay ahead took him into quicksand, where only his great momentum saved his life by propelling his sprawling body across the sand and water to solid ground. He clutched at roots and stalks of saw grass, pulling himself forward on his belly, writhing like a snake until he was free of the mire.

He lay still, spent from total exhaustion and fully expecting death to come at any moment. The night was hushed. He struggled to a sitting position and looked back. Nothing had followed him into the swamp. At least, nothing he could see or hear. Had his act of running generated his great fear and terror? He did not know. It was enough for the moment that he was alive. He did not want to think, to attempt to find any rational explanation for what he had seen and heard. The night had been stilled for only a short time. Rational thoughts could not return so soon! He lived only for these seconds of peaceful quiet, expecting that the whimpering might begin again the next moment.

He did not know how long he lay there before he got to his feet and staggered down the slough, conscious only of the fact that he must reach his horse. He came to a sharp bend and stopped in his tracks. He knew *something* was close by. He felt the warning but kept walking. His face twitched and he ground his teeth in his determination not to run in terror again.

A glimmering shape passed like a film of vapor over the saw grass to his left and then was gone. He would have liked to believe it was mist but was convinced it wasn't. His ears were alert for any sound from the Black but he heard no neigh or thud of hoofs. Then came a soft splash where there was no water, followed by a slight murmur in the saw grass.

He came to a halt, his eyes searching the night. Unfamiliar, floating fancies began to take shape; he shook his head angrily. He was creating images out of brush and saw grass that were absurd and past all reason! Had he gone so far that there was no escape from the captain's dark world of the supernatural?

He heard a single distinct note from a short distance

away and a chill ran through him that had nothing to do with temperature or weather. The note was repeated from a dozen different points in the saw grass, as if the night were filled with babbling voices.

The noise became an endless wail, a horrible, toneless, screeching cry of despair. His head was split with the sound of it, and yet he was unable to move, to run in terror as he had before. It seemed to hold him as if it were a solid mass through which movement was not only impossible but inconceivable.

The toneless wail wavered and babbled a few feet away from where he stood. It could not *be* and yet it *was,* he told himself. This was real and no nightmare. The danger was here and now! He smelled the sweet, sickening odor that had assailed his nostrils during his dream. It was not the stench of the swamp but that of human decay and death!

There was no movement in the saw grass, nothing to account for the source of the wail. His brain refused to accept the possibility that it was from anything human; it was too wild and terrifying to compare with any voice he had ever heard before. Yet, if he did away with all rationalism, he could detect separate and distinct notes forming the syllables *"Ko . . . ví,"* repeated over and over again.

With his acceptance of what he heard, a large shadow of unknown terror flashed before his eyes and communicated itself to his mind. He saw the grotesque faces and limbs and pieces of bodies that had appeared in the drawing.

He recoiled before the image of *Koví* as seen by the

captain's ancestors. Yet he could not run.

Suddenly the wailing stopped and the night was still. Peace came with the silence and Alec fought to rid his mind of the confusion and disorder, even the threat of madness, that were there. *There was no monster except what he created in his own mind! There was no horror except that which he was creating for himself!*

He accepted the fact that something was in the saw grass. It had not gone and would come again. He must face it but not on the basis of what he had ever seen or known before. He must not see what wasn't there. Terror would give way to a helpless panic that would drive him insane, as it had the captain. He could not escape. There was no turning his back to it.

A glowing mist, smoke-like in shape, appeared close by, clinging to the tops of the saw grass. It changed color from gray to luminescent gold.

Alec could not have taken his eyes away from it even if he had wanted to. For a few minutes it remained stationary, then it grew larger and began floating just above the saw grass, coming in his direction. It seemed transparent, for he could see the outline of something through it, perhaps the brush and grass beyond. It continued toward him, weaving an intricate pattern through the darkness.

Strangely he felt no fear of it and, stranger still, he was not surprised at his acceptance of it. It was as if a door in his mind had flown open and for the first time in a long while he was able to see and think clearly.

He knew the glowing mist was as real as the swamp around him. He had no preconceived ideas of what it could or could not be. He accepted it for whatever it was, whether it could be explained or not, by-passed or ignored. It did not exist in his subconscious but was before him, here and now.

He watched it glide toward him, luminescent and seemingly alive. It had no substance other than the tenuous smoke-like veil, no human or animal characteristics. It looked so temporary that it might disappear any moment and Alec believed that was one of the reasons he felt no fear.

He was not the first to look upon strange, inexplicable phenomena, he told himself. Sightings had been recorded for hundreds of years and the difference in them was only a matter of shape and speed. He looked upon the glowing veil, not knowing from where it came or why, only that it *was*.

It grew in size but no longer moved toward him. A scant twenty-five yards away, he gazed through its transparency and suddenly felt a renewed stirring of his fear. What he saw could not be. The open door of his mind clamped shut and, as his fear mounted, he sought desperately to open it again, to accept what he saw! The inner battle raged within him and the hair began to rise on the back of his neck.

There was an outline of a figure within the golden sheen. It was no monster but very small, more the shape of a child. As he watched, it became more and more distinct. He knew he had to close his eyes, that he could not look at it any longer.

Was he seeing something that wasn't there? Was his mind creating a figure that didn't exist at all?

He opened his eyes and found that the mist had not moved or grown in size; the figure was still present within its glow. There appeared something like a small human head, a faint outline of features. It resembled a child's face. The body was no more than twelve inches in size but perfect. It moved within the mist and Alec realized *it was alive!* It was his last rational thought before he lost all control and shouted in panic and terror!

With his scream, the small figure grew rapidly in size. Within seconds it enveloped the mist in its entirety and then, still growing, it burst forth, bright golden and suddenly monstrous to behold!

Alec saw what the captain had seen, that which he too knew from the drawing and his dream—a monstrosity, a misshapen head, a single green eye, jaws open and seeking. It moved toward him.

14 · The Bridge

Alec found that he could not move or take his eyes away. His stomach turned over in a great wave of terror, so powerful he vomited. He heard the rush of movement all about him; his head pounded wildly, his vision dimmed. He was blindly aware that there was no chance of escape. Nothing was left but a dull resignation to death. The very quality of death was in the air. He felt its dampness and clamminess like the hand of a specter on the back of his neck. It was as if some slimy thing was about to devour him. He wanted death to come quickly.

A golden radiance engulfed him. It came like a rushing, cresting wave in a storm-tossed sea. He was swept

141

forward in what seemed to be a great plume of fire that geysered skyward. Yet he felt no heat, no pain, nothing at all.

There was no sensation of anything but the sensation of the situation. It was as if he was suspended in air while the earth below erupted with detonations. He could see nothing within the brilliant light. He was devoid of feeling.

Suddenly the light was gone and he was staring into a black void. His thoughts came clearly despite what he had experienced. It was as if his mind alone had survived and now was apart from his body. He didn't know where he was but he seemed to know what was happening to him. His mind told him to expect something. He waited; not knowing what it would be, only that it would come. He felt neither fear nor panic any longer.

The thought occurred to him that he might be already dead. He felt no sadness, no emotion of any kind, simply an awareness that came from outside and flowed directly to his brain. There were no words to describe it. There was no reality. He lived, if he lived at all, in a great void of darkness and expectation. He would have liked to be able to look out from inside his mind to see what was coming. He had no idea if his eyes were open or closed and it made no difference to him. The black void was all.

Suddenly he was aware of a pinpoint of color in the darkness. It weaved an intricate pattern and he believed it was searching for him. He sought to help it find him. Anything, his mind told him, but eternal darkness. He concentrated on the light and watched it grow. Was it the end or the beginning? He wanted to know if he was alive or dead; only that seemed important.

The light changed color as it neared him, becoming a dark flowing redness that cut a deep swath in the void. He waited, unafraid. There was no place to go, nothing to use but his mind.

The redness flowed around him, more like a flooding tide than light. It rose steadily and he abandoned himself to whatever it held. His mind envisioned no monstrous figure of *Kovi,* no small figure of a child; he was aware of nothing but the redness of the light. As it wrapped itself about him, there came a simple awareness of being alive. He could actually feel the softness of the crimson light on his body. He raised a hand, groping his way through the light, and felt something that had the texture of *flesh!* He held onto it, knowing that whatever it was, it lived beside him.

His mind held no preconceived pictures of what was real and unreal. There was only quick and final acceptance of the fact that, somehow, he had bridged two worlds, one of dense matter in which he lived and a psychic world which nobody knew. What he held onto was from that other world, yet it was here and now. When he let go, it would go back *there.* It would remain as long as he accepted it and knew no fear. All this was clear in his mind, and with it came an awareness, too, that his own fate hung precariously between these two very real worlds. If he became afraid, he would see the most monstrous of beings and the end would come swiftly, not of his physical self but of his mind.

Then he heard a sound. The sad and forlorn whimpering came from everywhere, filling the void with a remorseless wail. He tried to shut his ears to it, and his breath came in great rasps with his effort. His fingers closed about the flesh-textured crimson light, as if holding on to the hand of a friend. He would not let go! He believed that which he could not understand but was as real as his own world. He would not be afraid!

Feelings he could not describe came to him from all directions, flowing, descending, penetrating his very being until they became a single physical sensation, that of a fierce dark wind blowing on him, through him, reaching into his very soul. There was no longer any crimson light, just darkness. Yet he was not frightened. Nor did he feel pain or concern, only great peace and contentment.

Time that seemed an eternity passed. He was floating in a world that was completely new but he couldn't describe it, only that he was there and happy. The distant music he heard came as no surprise to him. It was as if he had expected it all along.

The notes were soothing; he knew now there never had been anything to fear from them. How childlike had been his terror because his mind had been closed to what could and could not be! Now he knew there was a *vaster reality* that lay beyond.

He listened to the familiar music, played as no orchestra could have played it. When finally it ended he heard the murmuring of an unseen audience. He wondered who they were and he searched the darkness for them in vain. There were no restrictions to his movements and he moved about as he pleased. He was not worried or concerned. It was a warm and friendly place.

An ethereal grayness attracted his attention, and he moved toward it. He saw the outlines of shapes and figures but no faces. He hurried forward, wanting to know who they were, not what they were doing there.

Suddenly he stopped. He did not belong with them. There was no fear within him, only an awareness that the grayness within the void was not for him. He backed away quietly. There was no need to see any more. He was free to go. There were no restrictions. He had only to believe in the bridge. There was his world and the other. He had nothing to fear from either of them. If he believed that, the bridge would always remain.

He backed away until he could go no farther. The dark wind began to blow again but it was not the same as before. It did not bring with it peace and contentment. It did not flow and probe deep into his very being and soul. It was a purely physical sensation, bringing coolness to a warm night.

He lifted his head and smelled the rotting stench of the swamp. His vision cleared and he saw that he lay in the middle of a slough, his clothes and flesh matted with muck and slime. A faint grayness appeared in the darkness, but it was not the same as before. It was the first light of dawn, cutting across the eastern sky.

He got to his feet and looked at his torn clothes and the mud caked on his hands. He had no doubt that what he had experienced was as real as this. He didn't try to understand what had happened but accepted the reality of it.

There was nothing he wanted now but to find his

horse. How long had he been there? Only moments that had seemed an eternity? Was the Black nearby? Could this be the slough in which he had seen him from his perch in the oak tree? He listened but heard nothing. Then he whistled repeatedly until the night was filled with his calls to the Black.

An answer came from the far right, a muted whinny followed by a whistle as high-pitched as his own. He left the slough and plunged into the saw grass in the direction of the call. He ran unmindful of any danger that might lurk in the grass. He felt none of the sharp barbs that opened new wounds. Nothing mattered but to reach his horse and he ran like a wild thing.

When Alec reached the next slough and found the Black waiting for him, he ran forward and rubbed his face against the warm dark coat. He said not a word but closed his eyes, knowing by the touch and smell of his horse that he was home.

15 · The Way Back

Moments later, Alec stepped back to look at his horse.
The long lead shank had become entangled in a swamp
bush; he tore it loose, believing it had been caught often
and had slowed down the Black's movements. He saw the
long running wounds made by the razor-sharp saw
grass. The Black's mouth was red-raw and there were
swamp burrs in his mane and tail. None of this mattered.
He was alive and together they would find their way
back.

"Come on," he said. "We're getting out of here."
He found himself shaking, trembling, so he did not
mount immediately. It was a natural reaction to what

he had gone through, he told himself. In a moment it would pass.

He glanced up at the Black's head. It was held high, the great eyes alert and peering into the night. Alec touched him and the Black responded with a twitching of his skin; it was as if they were two ghosts talking to each other.

Alec told him that there was nothing they could not overcome together. They belonged in a secure world, regardless of what dangers might lie in their homeward path.

The early morning breeze grew stronger, stirring the Black's mane and forelock. He remained still, his ears pricked up, listening to no sound that Alec could hear, scenting everything in the air. The Black was ready and alert for whatever might come.

Alec waited, knowing his own senses could not match those of his horse.

Finally the soft skin beneath his hand ceased twitching and Alec knew it was time to go. Whatever danger the Black had sensed in the night had gone. He took hold of the stallion's mane and backed up a step before moving forward to spring up with all the strength he had left. His body rolled and twisted as he reached his horse's back and gained his seat. Whatever happened from now on, he didn't intend to leave his horse.

His legs closed about the Black. "Let's go," he said softly.

Alec decided to ride to the clearing and try to convince the captain that there was nothing to fear from *Kovi* except the terror which his own mind created. If he could get him on his feet, he might be able to get him up on the Black. Then they could ride double.

Before them were the natural dangers of the swamp but no more than that. He was no longer in a state of utter helplessness. He had the Black; he did not feel remote and lonely any more.

He rode the Black at a slow and cautious walk down the dry slough until he reached the high ground of the hammock. Beyond was the clearing in which he had left the captain, but he saw no sign of him.

He dismounted when he reached it but held onto the Black's lead shank for fear of losing him. He walked around the edges of the clearing, his eyes searching the heavy growth while shouting at the top of his voice, "Captain! Where are you? Can you hear me?"

There was no answer and he stood quietly, wondering what he should do. The captain had been too ill to have traveled far. Where had he gone?

Alec covered every foot of the ground searching for a sign. He found the small gold figurine and picked it up, turning it over in his hands. The green jade eyes winked back at him, as they had when he'd first looked at it. He studied the large evil-looking head and the twisted body. His anger mounted as he held it in his hands. To think that this ridiculous object could create terror in a man's soul!

He drew back his arm to hurl it into the depths of the dark water. Then he checked himself, recalling what he had learned only a short while before and was forgetting so soon.

The figurine was only a symbol to the eyes of the beholder. One could make of it what he wanted, see what he chose to see. It held no unique charms or powers other than what existed in one's own mind. It was a nothing, like every other talisman. The secret lay in looking into one's own mind, not at the figurine.

Alec shoved it in his pocket, determined to find the captain.

16 · Koví *Strikes*

Alec retraced his steps over ground covered before. Nothing stirred in the night but the clicking of the Black's hoofs at his side. He descended into a palmetto hollow and there found footprints, large and deep and fresh, made by running feet.

Alec had no doubt they were the captain's tracks. But what had given him the strength to run? Alec had left him in a state of complete emotional shock, unable to speak let alone get to his feet and flee—*from what?*

Alec followed the prints across the hollow and into the brush. He walked cautiously, ever on the alert for any sound. A fine mist drifted from the swamp with

151

the coming of dawn. It was clammy and for a moment Alec felt uneasy. He stopped abruptly and patted the Black, finding reassurance in his company.

The captain might be running from the horror of his own creation, the monstrous *Kovi*. That would account for his panic and superhuman effort that enabled him to rise to his feet and run for his life. Alec could think of no other explanation.

He walked on, following the footprints through the heavy underbrush and wondering if he would be able to convince the captain that his terror of *Kovi* was only in his *mind*. A streak of silver was visible above the tops of the trees. Soon it would be light enough for him to find his way home with or without the captain. He was traveling in the right direction and for all he knew the captain might already have left the hammock. He thought he saw a small bright spark glittering above the trees a short distance away, but it disappeared so quickly he couldn't be sure. He continued watching for it, but it didn't reappear. It could have been anything, he decided—a firefly, perhaps a shooting star.

Alec walked on through the mist with the Black close behind him. Gloom and darkness still held the hammock but he no longer needed to follow the captain's footprints; his trail was clear in the heavy brush where stalks of plants lay bent and broken.

Alec came upon an area where the brush had been flattened to the ground by the full weight of the captain's body. Had he rested or fallen? There were clumps of uprooted sod lying in every direction. Alec picked up one of them and found it wet and smelling of blood.

What had happened to cause the captain to tear this sod from the ground and apparently hurl it about? Had his terror become so great that he believed he was defending himself against *Kovi?*

This was not too difficult for Alec to imagine. In his own panic he had seen the monstrous form of *Kovi.* Yet he must face the situation as it *was,* not as he *imagined* it, he told himself. Neither *Kovi* nor anything else could actually materialize.

Yet had he not touched something within the crimson light that had the texture of flesh? What was the truth? Alec asked himself. *Was the answer a form of death itself?* He didn't know.

Alec came to a familiar grove of large trees and knew without doubt that the captain was returning the way they had come. He brushed aside the thick veils of Spanish moss. At the base of a large oak tree the captain lay sprawled on the ground, face downward.

At first Alec believed him to be resting, even sleeping. "Captain," he said. "Wake up."

Alec drew back in horror when he saw the blood draining from beneath the man's head. He turned him over and his shock was complete.

The captain's eyes were open but they were the eyes of a dead man. His mouth had been struck or kicked, for his lips were severely battered and all his teeth were smashed in. Something had happened to his hands, too, for they were torn and covered with blood; the fingers were curled, as if he was still clutching, reaching for an object of terror!

Alec looked into the ravaged face with the unclosed

eyes staring at him. Had the captain been right and he wrong? Was *Kovi* more than a mental image created in the mind of the beholder? Could he materialize and inflict these terrible physical blows?

The captain's eyes were filled with unbearable agony, not the agony of pain but that of fear too great to bear. They affected Alec as they never had done when the captain was alive, and yet these were dead eyes.

Alec found he could not take his gaze from them. They held him as if he and the captain had been linked together on the borderline between the living and the dead . . . as if each had gazed at something which had strayed from another kind of life into their own, something they could not comprehend, something that did not belong.

The lead shank was taut in Alec's hand and he realized suddenly that the Black was trying to break away from him. He tore his eyes from the captain to control his horse. The Black's nostrils were flared and his ears were pinned back.

Alec moved him away and then turned back to the captain. What should he do, he wondered, leave and go for help? What kind of help? The captain was beyond anything a doctor could do. Yet others must be informed so the captain's body could be removed from the hammock. The police would have to know what had happened.

But what *had* happened?

Alec looked down at the ravaged figure sprawled before him. Who had struck the physical blows, if *Kovi* had not materialized bodily? He saw the trail of dark bloodstains on the trunk of the tree, the bark torn off in great pieces. He looked again at the captain's blood-covered hands. Had he in self-induced frenzy clawed the tree in an attempt to escape his awesome mental image of *Kovi?* Had he, a superstitious imbecile, in his terror, pounded his head against the tree, using his great strength to inflict blows upon himself in preference to the horror which appeared before his eyes? Could that be the answer to what had happened?

Alec looked into the captain's wide-open eyes that, even in death, did not know peace. He felt no fear of what he saw in them; it was no longer contagious. He had survived but the captain had not. His death had not come from the blows inflicted by his own hands but from his mind. It was a fearful thing to know that fear unchecked could kill.

Alec turned away. He would first tell Odin, then he would ride on to the ranch. It would take many hours at best, providing he could find his way.

The sky was lightening with the gray of early morning when Alec swung himself up onto the stallion's back. The night was behind him but he knew the horror would not be ended until the captain's body was removed from the hammock—and perhaps not even then.

17 · Nothing At All

Several hours later, the stallion's running hoofbeats shattered the midmorning stillness as Alec tightened his legs around him and sent the Black into a gallop. The worst of the muddy going was behind them and a short distance away the captain's hammock emerged from the waving sea of yellow grass.

The Black snorted and plunged forward, as if he too was glad to leave the swamp behind. He waded through the shallows at the foot of the high bank and climbed to the firm ground of the hammock.

Alec kept the Black at a run and, with the triple racing beat of hoofs in his ears, he found it increasingly difficult to believe that he had actually experienced the horrors of the night. In the misty sunlight filtering through the trees everything had a dreamlike quality to it.

He kept his head close to the Black's neck. Nothing had changed but the passing of night to day. Everything that had happened to him was as real as the warm skin his face was pressed against.

The house loomed before him and he slowed the Black, finally coming to a complete stop. He was surprised at the wariness that had swept over him when nothing could account for it. The house was as he had left it, the shapeless roof rising in the center to the pillared tower, partially hidden by the fronds of the cocoanut palms. There was nothing to be cautious about any longer, he told himself.

Alec let the Black go on, approaching the house at a slow walk.

"Odin!" he called at the top of his voice. It was only then that he saw the large padlock on the front door and the shuttered windows.

"Odin!" he shouted again, knowing that no one but the old man could have closed up the house during the night.

He did not take the time to run up the steps and pound upon the door. He rode the Black at a gallop toward the barn.

The barn was closed and padlocked. Where had Odin taken the mare and why?

Alec rode over to the barred but open window of her stall. It was incredibly deserted, as if no horse had ever used it. There was no wisp of straw on the floor, nor a smell of any kind, either of manure or feed or saddle leather. But in a far corner he saw a spear-tipped rod, the same one he'd seen in Odin's hand the day before.

Whatever reason Odin might have had for closing and abandoning the place before the captain's return, he had swept the barn unusually clean before taking off with the mare. That was all there was to it. He would not think otherwise, Alec told himself. He was determined to think only in terms of common sense. But he must have the help of others. He turned the Black away from the barn, knowing that the only course open to him was to get to the ranch as soon as possible.

Several hours later, Alec rode down the dirt road which led to the cultivated farmland beyond. He still had a long way to go but, knowing that the Black was as spent as himself, he let the stallion choose his own gait. His gaze followed the flight of several buzzards over the saw grass; they planed in lazy circles, rising ever higher in the sky in their hunting. Alec cast a glance toward the south, wondering if he would get back in time to save the captain's body from the winged scavengers.

There was a haze on the horizon, and at first he mistook it for heavy mist rising from swamp water. Then he saw thin spiraling wisps of smoke and knew that it was not mist but fire! A lightning bolt from the storm of the day before could have started it, to smolder in the black peat during the night and come to life in the fresh morning breeze.

Alec tightened his legs about the Black and the stallion's strides quickened. He urged him into a gallop, then a run, knowing there was a strong possibility the fire would reach the humpbacked hammock before their return!

He'd gone no more than a mile when he saw dust stirring in the distance. A few minutes later he was able to make out a jeep coming down the road. He slowed the Black immediately but he was too tired to feel greatly relieved. At last his grim solitude was coming to an end.

Joe Early, the ranch manager, jumped out of the jeep. "Where the devil have you been?" he asked, more angry than relieved, now that he'd found Alec and the Black. "We've spent all night looking for you." Two Seminole Indians sat in the back seat of the jeep.

"Didn't you get my message?" Alec asked wearily. "From an Indian named Odin."

"No," Joe said. He turned to the two men in the jeep. "You know him?"

"Yes, Mr. Joe," one answered. "He come from old Jake Potter's place. But he no Seminole, Mr. Joe. Odin part Carib, ver' bad blood. But we not see him in long time."

"They'd know if there'd been a message, Alec. They're from the village and the best hunters in the swamp. That's why I got them."

"It doesn't matter," Alec said. So Odin never had left the hammock; he'd been there all the time, watching everything that had taken place. Being as superstitious as the captain, he would have believed they faced certain death by going into the swamp. His first thought would have been to remove all evidence of anything but an orderly move and to escape himself. He'd have no trouble selling the mare for a price that would enable him to return to Haiti and live as well as he pleased.

"*Where were you?*" Joe asked again.

"I was with the man Odin lived with, a Frenchman, Captain Pluminel . . ."

"But we went there," Joe interrupted sharply. "It was closed up tight, shuttered and padlocked." He turned to the Indians again. "What time was that, boys, three or four o'clock maybe?" The men nodded and Joe turned back to Alec. "He must have moved out days ago, so how could you have been with him?"

"He's dead, Joe," Alec said. "Just let me tell you that and I'll explain the rest later. You've got to help me. We've got to go back."

Joe Early studied Alec's face, then said quietly, "You're not going anywhere, Alec, not in the shape you're in."

"But I left him, Joe! You've got to believe me. We went into the swamp last night to the hammock with the humped spine. That's where he died. I'll show you. You've got to help me, Joe," he repeated.

"You went all the way to the humpbacked hammock?" Joe asked incredulously. "I don't believe it, no one could. Even with all the drainage going on . . ." Then quickly he softened his voice, alarmed by what he saw in Alec's eyes. "We'd better get you home, Alec." His concern showed plainly in his face as he took Alec's arm. "You're in no shape to . . ."

Alec tore his arm away. *"You've got to go back with me,"* he said.

"Okay, Alec," Joe replied kindly, trying to quell the terrible urgency he saw in Alec's eyes. "But not now. I mean, not right this minute. You wouldn't want the Black to travel that distance again, would you? You've got to think of him, if not yourself. And we've got to get some guns an' a few supplies. I'm not going into the swamp without 'em."

"Then you'll go?"

"Yes, providing we can get Dr. Palmer to come along with us. If Pluminel is dead like you say he is, I ain't moving his body until Doc says so. That's the law. I'll call him soon as we get back. He'll be home at this hour. He'll come."

"You promise, Joe?"

"I'll do the best I can," Joe answered, "for everybody concerned. Now get in the jeep, Alec, an' lead your horse alongside. You look like you're ready to drop."

Joe drove the jeep while Alec sat beside him holding the stallion's lead shank. Joe went slowly, knowing that the horse's energy was spent, as was Alec's. He'd do the best he could, as he'd promised, but it wouldn't be what Alec thought it was. He'd get Doc to give Alec a sedative that would put him out, make him sleep even if he didn't want to.

He'd seen others, older and more experienced than Alec, succumb to the real and imaginary hazards of the Everglades at night. The 'glades did things to a person's mind unless, if he was real lucky, he found his way out.

Alec had made it, but not by much; another few hours and he would have been finished for good.

Alec touched his shoulder but Joe didn't take his eyes off the road to look at him. He didn't want to see any more misery than he already had.

"Did you know him, Joe?" Alec asked in a voice not much above a whisper.

"Who, Pluminel? Well, no, not really. I met him once, about a month ago, when he first rented old Jake's place. It had been closed for over ten years. I know because I've been trying to buy it that long from Jake's widow over in Immokalee. She won't sell because she knows all this land is going to be worth more than I'm offering her, once it's drained. Old Jake built the place himself and that was quite a feat. That hammock was pretty much inaccessible before the drainage canals were dug."

Joe smiled, trying to humor Alec and erase the glazed look he saw in the youth's eyes. "I only spent a few minutes with Pluminel that time. He didn't seem to want company so I left him alone. All I wanted to find out, anyway, was if he intended to buy the place. He didn't, an' that was good enough for me."

"Did you see his mare?" Alec asked.

"No. I didn't know he had one. But, like I say, I didn't stay long and didn't see what he had in the barn, if anything. Old Jake had built it for his workhorse, an aged gelding named Jelly Roll."

Joe Early glanced at the two Indians behind him. "How about it, boys, did you know the Frenchman had a mare out there?"

The Indians looked at each other, smiling as they nodded their heads. "Yes, Mr. Joe. We seen her," one said. "Maybe same thing happened to him that happened to Mr. Potter, Mr. Joe."

Alec turned quickly to them, then back to Joe Early. "What do they mean?"

"Nothing," Joe said. "At least nothing that has anything to do with what you're thinking. It's just one of their superstitious beliefs, some kind of a swamp god that protects the Indians from those who'd take their land from them. Personally, I think they made it up, hoping to keep us out of the 'glades. But they ain't got a chance, as you can see for yourself. We're moving in all right."

"But what happened to Jake Potter?" Alec asked.

Joe Early glanced at Alec. "Nothing that had anything to do with their swamp god," he said. "Old Jake had just finished building his place when a big hurricane hit the area. Most of it was under water for several days. Later, when we got to Jake's place, we found him sitting on his horse in the barn. He was dead but Jelly Roll was still alive. We figured Jake climbed up on him to avoid the rising water and suffered a heart attack or something. His face had a pretty frightened look to it so we figured he'd suffered a lot of pain just before he died. The Indians with us looked on it as something else. They believed old Jake had been scared to death by their swamp god. They're a superstitious lot, Alec. When they talk that way you just ignore them."

Alec said nothing and Joe hoped the matter had ended. He wanted to get Alec back to the farm without any trouble. He owed that much to Henry Dailey, whom he'd promised to look after Alec while the trainer was up north. Luckily, Henry wasn't due back for another couple days and by that time Alec and the Black should be back to normal. He wouldn't tell Henry what had happened. He'd leave that to Alec. After a good sleep, Alec would realize that nothing that had happened to him in the swamp was real, *only imaginary*.

Joe glanced at the swamp through which the road ran. It was a horrible place and worthless before the Army engineers had arrived on the scene. Now it was only a question of time before the swamp was completely drained and it became rich, productive farmland and residential developments. Some people, mostly biology professors and nature lovers, wanted to save the Everglades, but not him. He was only interested in saving dollars, same as the real estate boys. He was going to get all the money he could out of the swamp.

Fires always helped speed things along and he welcomed the one he'd seen to the south. The yellow dry grass was ripe for burning. He turned his head to look at the smoke; it was more dense now, billowing ever higher in the sky, and coming this way. It was going to be a big one with a strong breeze blowing from the southeast. Nothing in its way had any chance of survival. Later, when the fire was out, the engineers would move in with their bulldozers and draglines.

Joe Early focused his eyes back on the road. Even if he'd wanted to go back with Alec, they never could have reached the humpbacked hammock before the fire. The whole area would be an inferno in no time at all. Anyway, it was ridiculous to believe Alec had left Pluminel there—or, for that matter, that he'd been with him during the night. He'd suffered hallucinations produced by sheer terror at being lost in the swamp. Joe didn't blame Alec. It could happen to anybody in the 'glades at night. It was best forgotten and he hoped Alec would get well soon.

The ranch was just a short distance away and Joe heard the Black whinny to the broodmares in the nearest pasture. He smiled. What he'd give to own that stud! Tired as the Black was, he'd run for the mares if given a chance. But they weren't for him, not now. In a few weeks, the big horse would be racing in New York.

Joe glanced sideways at Alec. He was slumped down in his seat, with his eyes closed. It wouldn't take much sedative to put him out for a long while, Joe decided. He'd be as good as new when he woke up; it'd all seem pretty much like a dream to him. Anyway, Alec wouldn't have much time to think about it, not with Henry Dailey coming back so soon. There'd be nothing but training and racing and work—the best thing for him under the circumstances.

Joe took a long breath and exhaled slowly. He'd sure like to see Alec and the Black race in New York but his job was here where nothing much ever happened. Well, the least he could do was to make certain Alec got all the rest he needed; that way he'd play a part in the big scene of racing.

18 · Race Day!

Four weeks later on April 19th, Alec Ramsay rode the Black postward at Aqueduct Race Course in New York City. It was the Toboggan Handicap at a distance of six furlongs for a purse of twenty-five thousand dollars.

They were last in the parade of five horses, a field kept small by the Black's entry in the race. He was the heavy favorite and carried high weight of 130 pounds, enough weight to give the others a fighting chance to beat him in his opening defense of the Handicap Championship.

Alec felt the first drops of rain from the ominous sky overhead. The heavy clouds let go quickly and the rain came down harder until he could barely make out the starting gate and the horses approaching it. Lightning flashed in the distance, followed by loud thunderclaps.

It would be a long time, he thought, before thunder and lightning did not take him back to a stable in the Everglades. It didn't matter that no one, not even Henry, would believe what he'd told them of that night. They had accepted only what they wanted to believe, all based on the medical testimony of Dr. Palmer that delusions were common to people under stress. He was glad he had not thrown away the gold figurine that night. They would accept that he'd found it in the swamp but no more. And, since he'd been unable to offer any *rational* explanation of the captain's death and his own horrible experiences, he had pretended to accept their version, if only to bring peace to his mind as well as theirs.

For several days afterward, he had been kept quiet by drugs. He held no bitterness toward Joe Early and the others, knowing it had been for the best. His dread of that which defied all common sense would not have enabled him to think clearly. Finally, the weight had lifted from his mind and he had looked upon the Everglades again.

As far as his eyes could see, there was nothing but smoldering ashes. The immense swamp to the south and west had been gutted by the raging fire. At his insistence, they had gone to the humpbacked hammock, more to appease him than to give any credence to his story. They'd found nothing, for no remains of the captain's body could have withstood the cremating blast of the holocaust. Still, he was glad that he had returned if only to prove to himself that he had been there.

He had welcomed the hard routine of work that followed. It was only occasionally now, always at night, when the odor of the swamp came to his nostrils and he dreamed a dream of a lost world, of images forgotten and yet not forgotten, all dwelling in dark places. He had no doubt that the dream would long haunt him, yet for reasons he could not explain he held no fear of it.

The Black suddenly bolted beneath him and his thoughts returned quickly to the job at hand. He peered through the half-light to see the milling horses behind the gate. The crewmen were trying to lead them into the starting stalls but the blinding rain only added to their burden.

Alec's strong, calloused hands were gentle on the big horse as he took him toward the gate. He knew the Black was ready, possibly stronger than ever. He'd be able to handle the footing with ease. Six furlongs was a short race for him but he needed the speed drill in preparation for the longer races to come.

Henry's instructions had been simply, "Just keep him out of trouble."

It wasn't always easy to follow orders, especially with the way the race was shaping up, with no letup in the rain and the track already deep in mud. He saw one horse skitter nervously across the track and bang into another. A race could be lost behind the gate as well as during the running of it, and the high weight on the Black made it doubly important that he remain quiet.

The minutes ticked away as the others entered the gate, then it was the Black's turn and Alec sent him forward. He walked very deliberately into the stall as if he knew the time had come for him to race.

The door slammed shut behind them and Alec awaited the starting bell. The Black was on edge, his high-strung nerves near the breaking point from his fierce spirit of competition. Alec made instant adjustments to suit the Black's quick movements in the narrow stall. Like his mount he was ready to go, legs raised at a sharp angle of knee to thigh, his back slanted, shoulders hunched, his muscles tense—everything required to send off the Black at the precise opening of the grilled doors. The long backstretch was before them with only one turn to round.

The starting bell clanged in Alec's ears and the race was on! The Black gained full stride almost instantly and Alec leaned forward above the plunging forequarters.

"Yah! Yah!" he shouted, his voice but one of five riders urging their horses to move still faster and break free of the most dangerous of all traffic jams, one of pounding, steel-shod hoofs!

Alec's arms were nearly wrenched from their sockets as the Black raced through the beating rain and semidarkness. Alec attempted to keep him on the outside and clear of the others who were packed much too closely together in a milling tangle of horses and riders.

Some were having trouble getting hold of the track and slipping dangerously. He saw one go down in the slop, his jockey somersaulting over his head. Then the Black was slammed hard by a big chestnut horse.

The Black bobbled and Alec helped him regain his balance; he steadied him and went on, clear of the tangle of horses. Two were still in front but Alec was not worried about catching up to them. The Black's feet were holding in the slop and if he made no mistakes guiding him, they would win.

Alec watched the rider on the second horse try to grab the lead by squeezing through a narrow opening on the rail. The opening closed just as the jockey started through it and he was forced to drop back or be slammed against the rail. He checked his mount, knowing his gamble had not paid off.

Alec drove the Black alongside him, keeping him hard on the rail. The Black was anxious to go on but did not fight Alec's hands. The pace was fast but he ran so smoothly that he seemed to be loafing.

Alec listened to the thunderous hoofs all around him and tasted the rain and mud flying in his face. He wanted no other kind of life but this, riding a fully extended horse against other jockeys, who were trying as hard as himself to win! He let out the Black another notch as they approached the far turn and drew alongside the leader.

Alec changed the Black's lead to the left leg going into the turn, and then let his horse run as he'd wanted to all along. For a few fleeting seconds, the other jockey did his best to stay alongside. He rocked, pushed and whipped, did everything he knew how to do to keep his mount going. The Black swept by, his long legs a blur in the rapidity with which they moved. He went around the turn with ever-increasing speed and entered the home stretch alone.

The crowd knew there was nothing more to the race but the electrifying stretch run of the champion. More than seventy thousand fans rose to their feet and gave the Black a tumultuous ovation as his hoofs beat thunderously in the slop, sending the mud flying behind him all the way to the wire. He had returned to New York victoriously and was once more on his way to racing glory!

An hour later, with the Black cooled out and in his stall, Henry Dailey joined Alec in the tack room. He handed him a folded newspaper and said, "I didn't want you to see this until after the race."

Henry had the same rider's build as Alec, most of his weight being in his arms and chest. He was portly but not fat, and as he moved about the room his gait had the smoothness and certainty of a much younger man.

"It looks like you were right about *The Ghost*," he added quietly, "that much of your story, anyway."

Alec read the large advertisement for the opening of the Ringling Bros. Barnum & Bailey Circus that day at Madison Square Garden. There was a long list of acts but only one had been circled in pencil by Henry.

THE GHOST—an ethereal horse act that will chill you, thrill you, leave you breathless with excitement and anticipation! Never before seen in America!

"Or maybe it isn't the same mare," Henry suggested.

"It's she, all right," Alec said. "Odin sold her, just like I figured."

Their gazes held until Henry turned away to get his floppy hat from a peg on the wall and clamp it down over his head. "Well, let's find out," he said briskly. "I thought you'd want to make sure. There's a matinée. I've already called the Garden and the act goes on about four o'clock. We can just make it."

Henry waited while Alec put on his raincoat. He'd never understand what had happened to Alec in the swamp, not completely anyway. In some vague way Alec had changed in appearance. He looked quite different but Henry didn't know exactly how. It was nothing he could put his finger on, just *different*. Maybe it was his eyes; they seemed to brood at times. Getting lost in the swamp at night must have been a horrible experience but Alec should be over it by now. He wasn't exactly sick but he wasn't himself either, not by any means. Alec had made no mistakes in the race today because his instincts, not his mind, governed his riding. But matters couldn't remain as they were. Perhaps seeing *The Ghost*—if it was the same mare—might help. Henry didn't know how but he was hopeful. He left the tack room, followed closely by Alec.

19 · The Greatest Show
on Earth

They left the towering glass-fronted stands of Aqueduct Race Course behind and walked up the steep ramp leading to the train station. A harsh wind had driven off the rain and it was blowing in such gusts that they bent double as they moved along. The huge ramp shook from the force of the blasts and signs swung crazily, threatening to rip loose.

"Crazy weather," Henry said, pulling his head deeper into the turned-up collar of his raincoat. "It's enough to drive a guy back to Florida."

Alec said, "I never want to go back there, Henry."

Henry felt suddenly alone again. They had shared

so many adventures together and now he felt like a stranger to Alec.

Reaching the elevated platform of the station, he held onto his hat as a gust of wind sought to take it from his head. He glanced at Alec, who stood straight and quiet beside him, his head bare and not seeming to mind the wind at all. His eyes were on the panorama of the New York skyline twelve miles away. Somewhere amidst all those buildings was Madison Square Garden and *The Ghost*.

The train slid into the station, the doors opening to admit the few like themselves who were leaving the track early. Henry was grateful that there was no need to push and scramble for seats. It had been a long time since he'd had such luxury in a New York subway train. The doors slammed shut and the train left the station.

They rode for a long while in a strained silence that made Henry even more uncomfortable. He was used to having things out in the open with Alec but who could believe such an incredible story as the one Alec had told him? Imagine anyone believing in a legend and search for a supernatural being named *Kovi!* It was enough to make one's hair stand on end just to have to listen to such a tale, let alone be asked to believe it! The best he could do for Alec, Henry decided, was to be patient and as agreeable as possible. Time would heal everything.

The train plummeted downgrade in the tunnel beneath the East River, its wheels screeching and grating in Henry's ears. He didn't have anything to say and was thoughtfully quiet. Perhaps nothing would come of this trip after all, just another horse act, but it was worth a try. Obviously the mare meant a lot to Alec. The train rushed into the 34th Street station and Henry got to his feet.

Shortly afterward, they left the crowded city street for the relative quiet of the Madison Square Garden lobby. The circus was half over and there were only a few late-comers like themselves buying tickets and moving to their seats.

Alec pushed on ahead of Henry; he'd glanced at his watch and found it to be a few minutes after four o'clock. An usher asked him for his seat stub but he went past without showing it; he wanted only to reach an aisle where he could see the center ring. Suddenly, a sound reached his ears and he came to an abrupt stop. Henry, hurrying to keep up, crashed into him and muttered an oath.

Alec heard nothing but the music. It came from the darkened arena and the notes were those he knew so well. He'd been prepared to see the silver-gray mare but the shock of hearing the music again made his blood run cold. He shivered in the darkness and his eyes became filled with the ice of his tears. *He was back in the swamp and his journey through it was as if he never had left.*

"Alec, what is it?" Henry asked, moving forward in the dimly lit aisle. There was no reply from Alec, nothing but a deathless stare into the arena where a gray horse moved about the center ring within the glare of a single spotlight.

Henry found that the air suddenly had become very

close. His skin that had been subjected all day long to wind and rain tingled as if with newly found warmth.

He listened to the music while watching the gray mare perform. His eyes became more and more excited as he followed her movements, recognizing them as those described by Alec. He found that it did not bother him greatly that this was just one more link in the chain that might bind him irrevocably to believing *all* of Alec's incredible story. He saw only the beauty of the gray mare, heard only the music swelling in his ears. It captivated him, as he was sure it must everyone else in the darkened arena.

There was no doubt he was watching a supreme exhibition of horse training. The gray mare was completely naked of saddle, bridle, halter or trappings of any kind. She was flawless in her movements as if some unseen hand was guiding her. Where did she get her cues, changing as she did from one dancing gait to another? Had Alec said that she'd been trained to the music?

He heard the peculiar piping notes that came and went, sometimes with a dreamlike slowness and barely audible, other times brisk and almost to the point of a horrible, shattering whistling. Simply by listening to the music, Henry found that he was willing to accept what he had denied before. The music created a feeling that *anything* was possible.

Breathlessly, since he was a trainer of horses himself, he watched the silver-gray mare as she floated about the ring. She paused with each syncopated step, dancing in measured cadence, supreme grace and beauty in every movement.

Henry knew little of the fine art of dressage but one did not have to know anything about it to appreciate such dancing! It was uncanny to think a man could have trained a horse to perform such movements alone!

There came a loud clash of cymbals, then the music faded, becoming more and more faint until it was almost impossible to hear. A strange feeling swept over Henry. He felt that somehow he was descending into a deep void and he didn't like it.

The music swelled, flowing around him. He was glad to hear the clash of cymbals again, for he did not like those muted piping notes. They made him uneasy, almost a little fearful, as if they meant something he couldn't understand.

To the roll of drums, the silver-gray mare sat back on her hind legs, balancing herself low to the ground while her forelegs were bent double. She held that difficult pose for several seconds before jumping across the ring on her hind legs and not coming down until she had reached the opposite side of the ring.

The music faded, leaving only the muted piping notes of the flute to be heard. They became louder and more shrill, creating the feeling that something terrifying was about to happen. They filled the darkened arena, and Henry could believe that they reached outside and beyond to the outer world of trees and stars and distant solitude. He shook his head to rid himself of such strange thoughts.

The notes were being made by a flute! he told himself angrily. They were ominous and yet they created a feeling of excitement and challenge. He wished they would end. He did not like being in the darkness, expecting something he did not wholly understand.

His eyes continued following the mare. She had responded to the flute notes by moving ever faster about the ring. She seemed to be seeking escape from them. For the first time Henry noticed a twitching of her ears, a quivering of her nostrils. She seemed terribly afraid or excited, one or the other. He could well understand her feelings.

Suddenly she sprang into the air with her forelegs and hind legs stretched out before and behind her. She appeared to be flying through the air, and Henry realized that this mare was the nearest thing the world would ever see to a winged horse, the mythical Pegasus!

He applauded loudly as the lights in the arena grew in brightness and brilliance. He had never seen such a performance in his life! The mare stood quietly in the center of the ring. The music had ended and Henry forgot everything but the pleasure he'd received in watching a superbly trained horse.

"Bravo! Bravo!" he shouted over and over again, beating his big hands together and making more noise than anyone else in the crowded arena.

The lights dimmed with the opening of the crimson curtain behind the ring. In an instant she was gone— like a ghost, Henry thought, her namesake. He clapped harder, hoping she would be returned for an encore, but was disappointed. The red-frocked ringmaster appeared and announced the next act.

Henry turned and found Alec gone. He ran for the stairs, knowing he'd find him with the mare in the stable area.

20 · Coming to the End

A circus guard attempted to stop Alec from going where the animals were quartered. He dodged him and continued running, determined to find the gray mare.

In the stable area, the circus animals and performers made for a scene of pandemonium if not confusion. Alec came to a stop, undecided which way to go, his eyes searching the area and the long corridors of temporary stalls for the gray mare.

He grabbed the arm of a juggler going by. "Can you tell me where I can find *The Ghost?*" he asked, shouting above the clamor.

The juggler shrugged his silk-clad shoulders and

smiled graciously. *"No inglés,"* he said. *"Habla español, señor?"*

Alec hurried on, making for the first row of temporary stalls. He caught a glimpse of Henry, fighting off a guard's clutching hands and coming after him. His steps slowed as he came upon a long column of matched chestnut horses being readied for the ring. While grooms adjusted feathered head plumes and jewel-studded bridles, a small man in dark evening clothes, holding a long whip, stood nearby.

Alec went up to him. "I'm looking for *The Ghost,*" he said, hopeful that the horseman spoke English and would be of some help.

"Yes?" the man said inquisitively, his eyes searching Alec's. "She is there in that stall. What can I do for you?" Despite his courteous words, his eyes disclosed his annoyance at being disturbed by a visitor.

Alec moved quickly over to a nearby stall. The mare was inside, her wet body being rubbed by a groom. What had he believed would be the outcome of finding her again—the end of his horrible nightmare? He remained stone still, watching her.

Finally he turned to the man standing behind him. "Where did you get her?" he asked.

"Get her?" the man repeated, further annoyed if not angry. "I do not understand you."

"She's not *yours,*" Alec said sharply. He saw Henry standing close by, motioning him not to lose his temper. He paid no attention to his friend. "Where did you get her?" he asked again.

Henry realized that Alec was one to be reckoned

with in his present mood. He'd seen him take risks on the track that had almost cost him his life at such times as this. Hoping to be helpful, Henry turned to the circus man, whose face betrayed no feeling of being discovered at deception or concealment of any kind.

"My name is Dailey," he said in a voice of complete authority. "Alec Ramsay here," he nodded toward Alec without meeting the youth's eyes, "has seen this mare before. He . . ."

"Oh, yes?" the man interrupted. "In Europe then. I, too, have just come from there. My name is Borofsky. I was with the Olympic Circus in Poland. You may have seen my Liberty act there?" His eyes brightened as he waved a hand in the direction of the chestnut horses being readied for the ring.

"No," Henry said. "I haven't seen it. I'll look forward to it." He paused but didn't dare turn to Alec. "It wasn't in Europe that Alec saw this mare, Mr. Borofsky. It was in Florida, a month ago."

The circus trainer turned quickly to Alec and there was a stark, almost frightened look on his face. His gaze held Alec's for several minutes, as if he searched for answers he didn't know himself.

Alec said, "She belonged to Captain Philip de Pluminel."

"Yes, I know," the man answered without hesitation. "One does not follow the circus in Europe without knowing of Pluminel. But is he not dead? I was told so when I bought her."

"From whom?" Alec persisted. "A man named Odin?"

The trainer's eyes became apprehensive again, even a little frightened. "Yes. He came to the winter quarters and asked for me, as I am in charge of all the performing horses in the circus. He had the mare with him and said that Pluminel had died en route there. He had the music for her act and knew about Pluminel's contract with Ringling. He asked me to buy her."

The trainer paused, smiling a little grimly. "It is true that I had some reservations as to Pluminel's death and this man, who claimed to be his great-uncle, having the right to sell her. But we were leaving on tour the next morning, and I had little to lose by taking her. It is not often that one is offered such a finished act."

Alec turned to the gray mare and, for a moment, seemed to be locked in his own thoughts. Finally he said, "I want to buy her from you."

"She is not for sale."

"At twice what you paid for her?" Alec asked.

The trainer laughed instantly and loudly. "Now I know you make fun of me," he said. "It is a joke, is it not? You do not know what I paid for her and yet you make such an offer! Why? You are not with the circus. What use would you have for her? And what if Pluminel is not dead and claims his mare? What then?"

Something strong stirred within Alec and he ignored the man's questions. "It is no joke," he said without anger or emotion of any kind in his voice. "Just tell me how much you want. I'll pay whatever you ask."

"Alec . . ." Henry began but was silenced by the look he saw on his friend's face. He knew he had to stay out of it, whatever reason Alec might have for making such a ridiculous offer to another professional horse-man. He turned to Borofsky, knowing well what was going on in his mind. It was an enviable position, one any horse trader would welcome. Henry kept his silence, telling himself to agree with whatever Alec decided to do. It would be worth it, if it helped, regard-less of the cost.

The circus trainer shrugged his well-tailored shoul-ders. "As I have said, she is not for sale and there is, of course, a contract to be considered." He paused, his eyes studying Alec again. "However, I suppose I could let her go and make all the necessary arrangements for . . . say a price of thirty thousand dollars. It is a great deal of money, I know, but she is very valuable as a per-formance horse. It would be easy for you to . . ."

"I'll buy her," Alec said abruptly. He turned to Henry. "Give me your check book, please."

"But Alec . . ."

"Please."

Henry handed Alec the check book, finding the whole thing overwhelming. He looked at the gray mare again. She was nothing they could ever use in their busi-ness. What possessed Alec? Why did he need this horse so much he'd pay the price of a top thoroughbred mare, one that would be worth something to them in the years to come? Henry shrugged his shoulders. It wasn't for him to answer. The last few weeks had been filled with impossible events.

Alec made out the check and handed it to Borofsky. "I'll send a van for her," he said, his patience exhausted.

"As you wish," the circus trainer replied, putting the check in his pocket.

Later, when Alec and Henry walked through the lobby of Madison Square Garden, the man said, "I guess you know what you're doing. You wanted the mare badly, that was pretty evident."

"I wanted her," Alec repeated. "I'll have her sent to the farm."

"For any reason in particular?"

"For a lot of reasons," Alec said, his voice so low it was barely audible. Seeing the mare again and listening to the music had brought back impressions and thoughts he'd been trying to forget. He needed to get outside and take a breath of fresh air, as rainy and miserable as the day might be. He felt as if he were going to burst with everything locked up so tightly inside him.

"I mean," Henry persisted, "would you have *any* reason I might be able to understand?" Then he added with attempted humor, "Even an old jackass like me likes to know what's going on." His eyes held a look of longing for answers he sought and had not found.

Alec came to a stop and put an arm around his old friend's shoulders. "There's one you'll understand," he said. "She's in foal to the Black, so how could I let her get away from us?"

A cold mask dropped quickly over Henry's face. "You mean," he said sullenly, "you let him . . ."

"I didn't let him," Alec said. "I couldn't stop it,

Henry. You refuse to believe what I told you about Captain Pluminel and that night, everything, just as if it didn't happen at all!"

Henry's eyes studied Alec's face for answers, then he felt an emotion stir within him that he'd never experienced before. Fear of what he could not understand swept over him. He could say nothing. He struggled, trying to find his voice.

Finally he said hoarsely, "You made up a ridiculous story for reasons I don't know or care to understand, Alec. I will repeat what I've told you before. I do not think it happened the way you think it did. You were lost and sick. Dr. Palmer said so, everybody said so. You had *hallucinations*."

"And if the mare has a foal," Alec asked, "will it be a hallucination too?"

"No, then I'll know you disobeyed my orders and bred the Black to her because you thought it would be a good mating. But I don't think Pluminel gave you a hard time. And I won't believe any crazy story about him dying the way you say he did. In fact, if you want to know something, I don't even think Pluminel is dead. Like Borofsky, I think he's going to turn up someday and claim his mare, then you'll have nothing to show for your thirty thousand dollars!"

"He won't show up," Alec said. "He's dead, Henry. You can believe that, if nothing else."

Alec had no trouble recalling the captain's pitted, staring eyes looking into his own; the smashed nose and mouth and broken teeth; the pieces of torn bark in his clenched hands and the trail of dark blood. He had died in self-induced frenzy and terror.

They left the building for the crowded street. The sky had cleared and the late afternoon sun could be seen above the Hudson River, too low to warm them but brightening their spirits nevertheless.

"Let's forget what happened and look ahead," Henry suggested. "We've got plenty of things to do this spring."

"I'd like that," Alec said, shouldering his way through the milling people on their way home from work. He was anxious to be one of the crowd. He wanted to get back to his horse and the work he loved. He wanted to do common things, entailing common thoughts.

His hand found the small figurine in his pocket and he wondered if it wasn't time to throw it away. Coming to a trash can, he stopped and took the figurine from his pocket. There was a throbbing in his temples as he looked at it. He had no fear of it, and yet he knew that with its coming his own world had altered. No single thing would ever again be quite the same as before.

Alec recalled the captain's words, *"I must never let it fall into strange, unkind hands."* He decided that he couldn't throw it away.

"Come on, Alec," Henry called irritably. "What's keeping you?"

"I'm coming," Alec answered. He looked at the figurine again; the green eyes appeared bright and seemed to be winking back at him. He put it in his pocket.

100